The
BILLIONAIRE
Full Disclosure

PETRA NICOLL

The Billionaire Full Disclosure

Published by Petra Publishing House
www.petrapublishinghouse.com

ISBN-13: 978-1-7340809-0-2

CHAPTER ONE

⸙

MAGICAL BIRTH

E li Evans rooted his head firmly against the seatback of a plush recliner in his Boeing 722 jet. He had hoped to be able to catch some shut-eye on the six-hour flight to Brownsville, Oregon from New York City, but he knew any efforts to relax would be futile. *I'm about to be a father!* he thought with exhilaration. All of the hours he'd spent in meditation, envisioning himself calm and grounded for this moment, seemed in vain. The mixture of excitement, anxiety, and pride he'd felt when first hearing the news of Angelina's pregnancy had now evolved into a full-on panic in anticipation of the birth.

I'll feel better when I'm there, he repeated to himself. In the meantime, he succumbed to visions of worst-case scenarios that now took on a whole different level of meaning as a soon-to-be-father. *What if the plane crashes, and I never meet my child? What if there are complications during the delivery that our midwife isn't prepared to handle and the baby doesn't make it…or Angelina? Or, what if everything with the delivery goes fine, but our child has a rare deformity…a third eye, or something?*

Eli chuckled at the last thought. *We should all be so lucky.* He'd been trying to cultivate a greater awareness of his own, invisible, third eye since having his attention brought to its existence a few years before. *What a ride this has been.* Eli welcomed the distraction a sudden flood of memories gave him from his anxiety.

Knowing that Angelina—the woman he loved more than he believed to be humanly possible—was at his childhood home in Brownville, Oregon along with his mother and grandmother caused a wide smile to grace his harried face. He couldn't wait to arrive at the farm he'd grown up on. *Too bad my dad can't be there*, he thought regrettably. *At least not in physical form.*

Neither of Angelina's parents would be there either, he realized, but that was by choice rather than impossibility. Eli had never met them nor spoken to them on the phone, even though they lived not far from their home in Los Angeles. Angelina never told him much about them either, save for the fact that her father was Indian and her mother American; he'd seen photos of them, wearing turbans.

She'd also told him that her young adulthood had been somewhat traumatic. She'd lived with her parents at an ashram where her parents still lived and where she'd had an enjoyable and educational youth, but uncomfortable teenage years. She'd shared that she'd left the ashram at the age of eighteen in order to avoid an arranged marriage. That's all he knew.

Angelina had called the ashram to notify her parents of her pregnancy several months before, but her news had been met with disdain. "We have no interest in meeting that child," her father had said. Her mother remained quiet, adhering to her husband's response. Their reaction had broken Angelina's heart and bewildered Eli, who had grown up in an extremely loving and supportive environment.

"Why are they so upset with you? How can they not be happy for you?" he'd asked after she hung up.

"It's complicated," was Angelina's reply.

"Yes, that much I gather, but for a religion that teaches the spiritual truths about love that you still practice today, aren't they being contradictory…and quite harsh?"

"A lot of the guru's teachings I still hold as my truth, and my parents do as well. But there are other philosophies that have been construed to meet his foundation's agenda."

"Which is…?"

"Well, let's just say it's a male-dominated religion. Like most religions, they are heavily concerned with growing their community, so their agenda upholds that intention. Men are given certain liberties that women are not…"

"Like what?"

"Do we have to talk about this now?" Angelina had become noticeably stressed. Eli did not want to add further discomfort to what had already been an emotional day.

"No, love. Of course not. I didn't mean to push you." He wrapped his arms around her and cradled her head in his hands like he would a child, for in her eyes, he saw for the first time the look of a wounded child. "I love you," he whispered. "And I love this child growing inside of you."

Angelina wiped away a tear that had started to form in her eye. "I love you, too."

Eli knew how blessed he'd been to have the parents he had. They'd raised him to know the value of hard work, to notice patterns in nature, and they had cultivated within him a passion for music. Both of his parents had been amateur musicians who had played in a folk band around Oregon. Eli grew up onstage. He was a natural musician and performer, but his parents had given him the opportunity to study advanced guitar and compose his own music—when his homework and chores were completed.

He was always a daydreamer and often complained in response to the farm tasks his parents had given him, but as an adult, Eli came to understand those responsibilities were critical in building the work ethic and stamina needed to reach the level of career success he'd reached. *They made me a rock star.* He emitted a sigh of disbelief. He'd never wanted to climb the corporate ladder. All he'd ever wanted to do was play music. But it still shocked him that he'd made it as far as he had. *I was born to perform,* he reflected. *And to raise the consciousness of the planet. And maybe even beyond...*

His thoughts started to drift back to the last conversation he'd had with Michael. *Ohmigod, that must have been eight months ago,* Eli thought. *How could so much time have passed without a visit?* Over the past few years, he'd reached out regularly to Michael—and Michael, of course, had often shown up unexpectedly; he was there whenever Eli had needed guidance. *I guess I got so swept up in preparing for the baby,* he realized. *Hmm...and maybe Michael wanted to allow me that time with Angelina. He always has his reasons.*

The thought of the baby jolted Eli back to the present. *God, the baby. I hope I'm not too late.*

He hadn't anticipated going back to Brownsville for another two weeks. The plan was to drive Angelina up to his mother's home from L.A. one month before her late-May due date, so she could relax in his mother's care and be near their midwife, Susie—the same woman who had helped his mother give birth to him. Eli was to meet Angelina there two weeks later, after completing his East Coast tour—the last stretch of road gigs before the three-month paternity leave he'd built into his schedule. But nature had other plans. Only three days after leaving Angelina at the farm and one day into his tour, his mother called to let him know Angelina was going into early labor.

"This baby is eager to enter the world," Carol had said. After assuring him that being born early wasn't necessarily cause for concern, she told him he'd better forget about the rest of his tour and get back on the plane. She spoke with a collected calm, but a sense of urgency. His manager would not be happy, but he'd long ago given up prioritizing profit over self-care and family time. *My fans will understand*, he thought. He had taken long stretches of time off in the past, and his fans had always come back. Besides, he wanted to lead by example. Everyone should follow their hearts and take care of themselves and their loved ones first. Even rock stars.

And actresses, Eli added. He was proud of the way Angelina had prioritized self-care during her pregnancy, even while at the height of her acting career. *My girl is in shape*, he thought proudly. She had the typical pregnancy cravings, especially for ice cream, but she knew it wasn't the ice cream itself that her body craved, it was something sweet and creamy. She kept yogurt and kefir and fresh strawberries on hand to quench the craving when it arose. Naturally, she kept up her yoga practice. She made the necessary adjustments to accommodate her growing belly, but he was amazed at her strength and dedication to a consistent practice.

Throughout the pregnancy, Eli and Angelina kept a nightly ritual of meditating together. Even if one of them was away, they joined together over the phone and set intentions for the child they were about to raise. They envisioned a healthy, strong baby; it didn't matter which gender (they wanted to be surprised). They asked for guidance in recognizing what the child's unique talents were so that they could nurture them. *Every baby is born with a purpose,* they'd acknowledge. *Remind us that the universe knows better than us what that is, so that we may surrender to it and not resist.*

Surrender. Eli reminded himself now, four hours before landing, that he couldn't control the outcome. He pictured himself at the farm, cradling his newborn baby in one arm and Angelina in the other, as his mother and grandmother looked on. That was the image that finally allowed him to fall asleep.

ELI AWOKE WITH a jolt. "What was that?" he said aloud, having forgotten he was on a plane.

"It was just the plane landing, Sir. You had fallen into a deep sleep," Sarah, his flight attendant, answered.

"Are we in Brownsville?" Eli rubbed his eyes and looked out the window.

"Yes, we are, Sir."

Eli was used to flying into Eugene, Oregon and driving the remaining thirty minutes to Brownsville, but special arrangements had been made to land at a small, private airport near Brownsville in order to save time. Sometimes it paid to be famous.

Eli hurriedly reached for his phone and turned the power back on. Several text message alerts went off. His eyes scanned the messages from his mother, his finger scrolling down until he reached the last one, sent only seven minutes earlier.

"Angelina is a champion. Eight hours into labor now... baby is getting closer!!"

"I haven't missed the birth yet!" he exclaimed, reaching for his bag and rushing to the door.

"Go, Eli, go!" Sarah and Tim, the pilot, cheered him on after it was safe to exit the plane. A driver stood ready, the door to his black Toyota Camry open. He threw Eli's bags into the trunk of the car and drove his anxious passenger the remaining four minutes to the farm, breaking a few minor traffic laws along the way.

As they pulled up the familiar driveway, Eli warned, "I'm getting out here. Pull over, pull over!" The driver knew better than to argue and quickly brought the car to a halt. Eli threw open the door and ran the remaining 200 feet to the house, ignoring the fact that he would have arrived at the door faster had he stayed in the car.

"Eli!" He already saw his mother open the front door. "Hurry!" There was no time for social formalities. He quickly squeezed his mother's hand as he charged past her, following the sounds of Angelina's moans.

The first-floor den had been converted into a nursery. Plants hung from the ceiling and sat in pots on the windowsill. A stream of sunlight stretched across the creaky wooden floor. A wooden crib was in one corner, a changing table in another, and a daybed along the wall. In the center of the room, Angelina sat in an inflatable pool of water, her arms behind her on either side, bracing her body against the pool walls. Eli couldn't tell if she was covered in water or sweat. Susie, the midwife, stood behind her massaging her neck and shoulders, but Eli paid her no mind as he rushed to Angelina's side and began kissing her face all over.

"My love, my love, I'm here, I'm here. That's my beautiful, strong woman."

Angelina smiled, breathing deeply. "I'm so glad you're here…"

"She's been wonderful, Eli." He finally noticed his grandmother, quietly seated in a chair in the corner. In her hands was an open book.

"Oma, hello," he smiled.

"Hello, dear. I've just been reading your Angelina some poetry. I read from this same book after your mother gave birth to you."

Eli looked back at his mother. There was so much history in this room.

"It's true, I remember," she smiled, reaching for the tincture of crampbark and chamomile that Susie had made for Angelina. "Here you go, dear," she held the mug to her daughter's lips.

"How are you, my love?" Eli looked imploringly at Angelina.

"Tired," she winked.

"Of course. Can I do anything to help?"

Angela's face winced as a contraction came.

"What's happening? Is the baby coming?" Eli started to panic again.

"Relax, Eli. We've got this," his mom grinned. His grandmother started to hum a song he'd remembered her singing when he was a child. The midwife guided her arms gently up and down Angelina's back and his mother laid a cold compress on Angelina's forehead.

The contraction resided. "Five minutes," his mother said.

"Five minutes until birth?" Eli asked.

"The contractions are five minutes apart," Angelina

looked at him curiously. "Don't you remember anything from birthing class?" she teased. Eli was grateful she felt well enough to still have her sense of humor.

"That must have been the week I missed," Eli winked.

Just then, a car could be heard coming up the driveway. "Are we expecting someone?" Eli asked, gesturing toward the window.

"Maybe…" His mother smiled and winked at Angelina and Eli's grandmother before rising to greet their guest. Angelina looked hopeful. Eli felt as though he'd been left out of a secret. He kissed Angelina on top of her head before rising to see who was at the door.

"Welcome, please, come in." He watched his mother warmly embrace a slender woman wearing a white dress and turban, with a green shawl draped over her shoulders. She was light-skinned; he guessed the color of her hair to be a light brown. Her eyes, however, were the color of coffee— pure Angelina. *Angelina's mother*, Eli thought, his mouth gaped open.

The woman shyly entered the room, eagerly searching for her daughter. "Is she okay?" she asked, her voice cracking slightly with nervousness.

"Yes, yes. Angelina is well. She is dilated at seven centimeters…contractions are five minutes apart now." As if on cue, Angelina could be heard releasing a moan, guiding her mother to the nursery, just as she'd guided Eli.

"My baby…" Angelina's mother's eyes welled up, as did her daughter's, as she gently approached the pool.

"Mother…" Angelina choked on the word, overcome with emotion. "I'm so glad you're here. The baby is almost ready." She squeezed her mother's hand.

Eli's gaze bounced from Angelina to his mother, his

grandmother, and finally their guest. *Who had arranged this?* he wondered. It didn't matter so much now, he realized.

"Elizabeth," he stood to greet her. "It is a pleasure to meet you. I am Eli."

Elizabeth turned toward Eli, her hands together in prayer. She nodded slowly, silently. If it weren't for the small smile across her face, Eli would have wondered if their meeting was, in fact, a pleasure. She seemed to want to reach out to him but something was holding her back.

She turned her attention back to Angelina.

"We are all here," Angelina spoke quietly, holding eye contact with her mother. The thought crossed Eli's mind that, not only was his father not present after his death nearly a year before, but Angelina's father wasn't there either. To his love, however, it was clear that those she had needed to be present, were.

The pain Angelina had been in with each contraction seemed to lessen in intensity; the presence of her mother calmed her. What happened next was a blur. Eli went from confusion and surprise to exhilaration. Angelina breathed deeply and barely released a sound as she gave one giant push and out from the water, gently pulled their child.

"My baby…" Angelina cried, repeating the words her mother had just said to her. She held the newborn up to her chest. "It's a boy," she sobbed.

"A son! I have a son!" Eli released his own tears of joy. He shared a knowing glance at Angelina that confirmed their baby now had a name. The midwife wrapped a towel around the baby, who let out a small cry, and placed him upright against Angelina's bare chest. Eli reached for the boy's tiny, delicate hand. "Hello, little Gabriel," he kissed his forehead. "You're okay. We love you." Eli turned to Angelina in amazement, "You did it, baby. I love you so much. You are amazing."

Eli could feel he had just been witness to the sacredness of the feminine. Around him were five powerful, spiritual, and wise women whose bodies and spirits knew how to create, nurture, and deliver the precious gift of new life. They knew so much more than him, he realized. *I can never know what they know.*

He missed his father, but he knew he had witnessed what just happened, too. Looking into his baby boy's eyes, he recalled what his father's spirit had once told him: "I chose you to be my son, just as you chose me to be your father. We all have that choice before a baby is conceived. We chose each other. We are soulmates, don't you see?"

Yes, I chose you, Eli looked into the squinting eyes of his child. *Thank you for choosing me. I promise you I will do everything in my power to make the world you were just born into the best that it can be.*

CHAPTER TWO

———— ⚬⚬⚬ ————

HEALING THE PAST

Angelina could not have been more grateful for her mother's presence at her baby's birth. She had been unsure if she would come. She knew Eli's mother had made a phone call to the ashram a few days before, making sure her mother knew she had an open invitation to visit. The rest was up to her.

Unbeknownst to Angelina, her mother had gotten off the phone and, in a moment imbued with emotion, asserted herself in front of her husband for what may have been the first time in her life. She was going to visit their daughter, with him or without him. She packed a small suitcase, loaded it in their beat-up old Chevy, and—upon not seeing any initiative from her dumbfounded husband—got behind the driver's seat and was off.

After spending one night at a hotel near Ashland, Oregon, she made her way to Brownsville. Pulling into the Evans' family driveway, she was pleasantly surprised. It was not what she'd expected, although she admitted she hadn't given her expectations much thought. When Angelina had told her she was in a relationship with a musician—a world-famous one, she discovered—she'd assumed his roots to have been far more extravagant than what stood before her.

It was a humble home; one that had been well-loved, that was certain. The landscape was beautiful; towering pines and evergreens surrounded the property and a creek ran right through it. The grounds were only lightly landscaped; splashes of color were supplied by gorgeous shades of bright pink and purple rhododendron blossoms. Spring was in the air.

The land looked as though it had been an active farm, until recently. The barn was well-maintained, but the doors were closed and there were no signs of animals inside. *I wonder what's in there*, she thought. She had little time to entertain her curiosity, however, as a much more important task was at hand—seeing her daughter and, hopefully not quite yet, her new grandbaby.

After being welcomed into the home, she knew she had made the right decision to come when her eyes met her daughter's. Something primal kicked in upon seeing her daughter about to give birth. An energetic pull took place—one that she had suppressed for many years. *I let my mind get in the way of my heart.* Her eyes welled up at the realization.

Then, it all happened so fast. She became a grandmother. And although she knew the midwife—and even Eli's mother—were eager to step in and assist, they both intuitively stepped back and allowed her to respond to her maternal instincts. With the baby resting upon Angelina's chest, Elizabeth could see that the newborn was already reaching to be fed. She placed her hand on the baby's upper back and neck to steady Gabriel.

"Rub your thumb and finger back and forth across your nipple and compress your areola, dear," she suggested to Angelina. "That will encourage some of your colostrum to come out." The scent of his mother's first milk led Gabriel to bury his chin into his mother's breast, open his mouth, and instinctively latch on.

Angelina lifted her gaze from her baby to her mother. "Thanks, Mom," she smiled. She knew how essential it was for her baby to absorb the nutrients in her milk; her colostrum contained antibodies to protect her son against disease.

The importance of breastfeeding had been taught at the ashram. Angelina had witnessed live births many times while growing up and watched several of those babies grow up. She understood that babies need to nurse for many reasons—security, bonding, and positive hormonal releases—but that it was healthy for mothers, too. It would help her body recover from pregnancy; the oxytocin released while nursing would trigger her uterus to contract, reducing post-delivery blood loss and helping it return to its normal size more quickly.

She also knew that breast milk has bioactive components that help in the optimal development and function of her baby's gastrointestinal tract, immune system, and brain, which is why she and Eli had held the intention of breast-feeding Gabriel for several months, if not years. Miraculously, the composition of her breast milk would change as the baby developed, ensuring optimal nutrition for that stage of his life.

But any moment in the future was far outside of Angelina's consciousness as she smiled sweetly into the squinting eyes of her newborn child. "You are our little miracle," she whispered lovingly. "And we love you so very much."

She looked up gratefully at Eli and around the room at the incredible women that surrounded her. She became acutely aware of an adult male presence as well, although she wasn't sure who it was. She didn't give the feeling much thought though—she was absorbed in the ecstasy of holding her child in her arms, his tiny little lips suckling nourishment from her body.

Angelina began to hum a Bajan song she had sung to her baby many times while still in the womb. It was one her mother had sung to her as a child. It served as a sort of calling to her mother; an opening. Elizabeth approached her daughter and placed her hand on her shoulder and began to sing. The room became quiet; everyone closed their eyes to absorb the moment. Angelina's voice joined her mother's and it was clear that something profoundly deep was passing through their bodies and into the newborn baby.

When the song ended, Eli opened his eyes and looked into Angelina's. What beauty lay before him. He was so grateful to have found this woman and to have her be the mother of his child.

THE NEXT FEW days passed in a cloud of unmarked dates and times. Gabriel kept Eli and Angelina up every couple of hours, if not the whole household, with his newborn needs. They couldn't imagine what new parents—especially single mothers—must go through if they don't have support. They were grateful to have the love, experience, and wisdom of both of their mothers nearby during these demanding and exhausting days.

Susie, the midwife, had left a few hours after the birth and Eli's grandmother returned to Idaho after a few days of cuddling her new great-grandbaby. Eli's grandfather had not been feeling well, and she didn't want to be away too long. Eli hired a driver to ensure she got home safely.

Carol and Elizabeth remained. They slowly got to know each other over laundry, cooking, and cleaning. It turned out they weren't nearly as different as either of them had anticipated. They both held strong spiritual beliefs—often in alignment—and a deep love for their children, albeit expressed in different ways. Carol could see how Elizabeth had a strong inner light that had been dimmed over the years, by her husband or by her guru, she wasn't sure which. Perhaps both. But Elizabeth didn't say much about them, and Carol wasn't the pressing type.

What was clear was that Elizabeth wanted to be closer to her daughter. The irony was not missed by either of them that years had passed with Elizabeth and Angelina both living near Los Angeles, yet the first time they'd seen each other in years was nearly one thousand miles away.

"You have a beautiful place here," Elizabeth shared as the two leaned over the kitchen farm sink, washing and drying dishes.

"Thank you," Carol smiled. "It was a gift from my aunt. As a child, I'd spend hours roaming the fields around here and reading by the creek. After my aunt passed, Robert and I fixed her up and kept her going as a working farm. We both loved animals."

"I didn't see any animals. Do you still farm?"

"Oh, no, not since Robert passed away last year. Too much work for this little old body," she winked. "Eli insisted on hiring support staff to maintain the land and home so I could stay here, but I decided to let the animals go. The cows and goats were only used for their milk anyway—and companionship, of course. Sweet souls they were."

Elizabeth smiled. "I'm sorry to be nosy, but I noticed your barn…it has an extraordinary life energy to it. Are you using it for something besides animals now?

"Ah! You are insightful. It does have a special energy, doesn't it? Eli helped me with that, too. We had it converted into a pottery studio. It's my little creative space now. I so love it in there. Would you like to see it?"

"I…well, yes, I would."

Carol dried her hands on a towel, the last of the dishes washed. "Very well. Let's go!" The women peeked into the nursery on their way out. The newborn was nursing peacefully in his mother's arms. Eli was taking a nap on the daybed, and Angelina gently smiled to signal they were doing fine.

The ladies walked the fifty-foot gravel path to the barn, taking in the sweet smell of pine as they ambled along.

"We planted that tree over there for Eli's first birthday. Can you believe how tall it's grown?" Carol signaled to a towering white pine tree near the creek. "It has to be over fifty feet tall now," Carol glanced at Elizabeth. "They grow so fast, don't they?" Elizabeth knew Carol wasn't just talking about trees. She felt a pang of guilt for the years of her daughter's life she had missed, but she said nothing about it.

Arriving at the barn, Carol gave the door a gentle push and welcomed Elizabeth inside.

"Here we are!" Carol's face beamed with pride.

"Wow…it's…" Elizabeth was at a loss for words; the space was so vibrant and earthy. Painted ceramic tiles decorated the walls in every shape, color, and pattern. Finished pieces adorned shelves—vases holding fresh flowers, fruit bowls holding fresh fruit. Additional shelves held yet-unglazed mugs, plates, and decorative platters.

Maybe it was the smell of the clay that made Elizabeth feel grounded or the intimacy of being invited into Carol's private space, but she suddenly felt compelled to open up. Tears began to well in her eyes as she turned toward Carol, "How do you do it?" she asked.

"How do I do what, honey?" Carol knew the question wasn't about her art.

"Don't you get lonely? After Robert died?"

"Oh, dear, yes of course. I miss him so much. But I am doing what he would have wanted—finding joy and peace in this new reality of life without him."

"I…I can't imagine life without my husband. I mean, he travels regularly, but he always comes back. And there are expectations he needs me to fulfill for him while he is away. And when he is home…well, there is even more I must do. I forget sometimes…who I was before him, you know?"

Carol held the space for Elizabeth's vulnerability.

"I was a strong woman, I know that. And a nurturing and protective mother. Until…" Elizabeth began to sob. No words could escape amid the ambush of tears. Carol approached and put her arms around her.

"You are still a strong woman, Elizabeth. Whatever happened between you and your daughter, it can be healed. You are healing it now, just by being here."

Elizabeth's vision was blurry, but when she looked up into Carol's eyes, she was surprised to see so much love from a woman she had just recently met. She could only imagine how much love this woman must have poured into her child.

"I look forward to getting to know your son," she said sincerely.

"You are always welcome here," Carol smiled. "You are family now."

Eli had heard that the feeling of holding his newborn baby would be indescribable, and that was certainly true. The closest he could get to defining it was to think of a giant pot of soup. He knew that every emotion stemmed from either love or fear and that the emotions that were given the most thought and intention were what would manifest in his life. In this pot of soup were joy, elation, bliss, ecstasy, adoration, fascination, pride, awe...the list went on with key ingredients of this sort. Sprinkled in were also panic, exhaustion, and uncertainty, but these emotions were over-powered by the other flavors. The soup was simply named "love."

For a while, he could not differentiate time; there was either daylight or darkness, awake or not awake (and far more of the former). Angelina carried the bulk of the weight, he was aware. Feeding their child was entirely de-pendent on her, although he did what he could to soothe the baby when he cried and to change his fair share of dia-pers. He was amazed by the boy's little fingers and toes and tiny little blonde hairs on his head, but even more amazed by the strength of his wife.

She had made the birth look easy, though he knew it was anything but. She also seemed to glow even when op-erating on days of little to no sleep. He hadn't thought he could love her more, but after seeing her nose and shape of her chin reflected in their son, he saw her in a whole new light. She had made him a dad. And she had done so with beauty and grace.

"How are you, love?" he asked her now, what he assumed to be nearly a week after the birth.

"The same as I've been every day—completely enamored with our little one. And with you," she winked. "I think he'll have your hair and eyes."

"And my dashing good looks?" Eli smiled.

"And your inflated ego?" she joked back.

"I hope he has your heart," Eli replied.

"He has our heart, love. One and the same."

"I think you have your mother's heart, as well." Eli didn't know the chain reaction his words would spark.

"What do you mean?"

"I mean, your mother seems very kind and loving. She's a good woman. I don't understand what kept you both apart so long."

"No, you don't understand."

Eli, in his exhaustion, registered her anger a little late. "Okay, I guess I don't. So, tell me about it. You're always so secretive."

"You're seeing the best side of my mother. Did you notice my father isn't here?"

"Yes, of course."

"She's a different person around him."

"How so?"

Angelina hesitated, as she always did when approaching this subject. Seeing her sleeping child in the cradle before them, however, this time she knew she needed to share this part of her past with Eli. She had pieces of herself she had to heal, or else they would inevitably be passed down onto their child.

"Men have particular roles in the ashram I grew up in. As do women. I didn't realize how dangerous those roles are until I turned seventeen." Angelina paused as Eli listened patiently, not wanting to break her stride. He'd waited years for her to open up about her past.

"My dad wasn't around a whole lot during my childhood, but he had the strongest presence. I don't know if it was a matter of how he was raised in India or influences from the ashram—most likely a mixture of both—but he had certain expectations that he placed on my mom, and later on me. I told you theirs was an arranged marriage, right?"

"Yes, you did."

"And that they wanted the same for me?"

"Yes, you told me."

"It's like he—and other men at the ashram—wanted to raise strong, intelligent, and intuitive women, but as soon as they would get married, they wanted those qualities to be replaced by those of a 'dutiful wife'—someone who would cook and clean and dote upon them without complaint. Someone who…would please them sexually at any time, in any way they wanted."

Angelina's voice cracked, as though choking on a memory. Eli pulled up a chair and sat beside her, his hands holding hers gently but firmly.

"Boys…even boys were taught that the woman they were to marry was to be their property. If it wasn't said explicitly, it was said by example. Women didn't say 'no' where I grew up. Until I did." Tears formed in her eyes.

"It's okay. You are safe here," Eli kissed the top of her head.

"The man…the boy, really…that I was supposed to marry—that my parents and the guru chose for me to marry—he thought he owned me. He didn't show that side to my parents, but I saw the writing on the wall from the beginning. I don't know how they didn't. One night, everything erupted. I went to a private yoga room, just like I did every evening to prepare my body and mind for bed. He knew…he knew that I practiced for an hour in there alone.

"And he came…that night, he entered quietly, when my eyes were closed and I was lying in Savasana. I had music playing, and I did not hear him come in. The next thing I knew, he was on top of me. During my most sacred time with God and my body, he held me down and entered me. I didn't even have time to scream, but I know I said no. I know I said no…"

Angelina let out a wail that woke the baby. Carol and Elizabeth came rushing to the nursery, alarmed. Carol reached for the baby, cradled him in her arms and left the room to calm him. Elizabeth stood frozen in the doorway, sensing her daughter's desire for her to maintain her distance.

"You let him get away with it!" Angelina yelled at her mother through tears, as though that moment nearly ten years ago was just yesterday. "You didn't protect your own daughter!"

Whatever bond that had finally seemed to be growing back between Angelina and her mother was suddenly broken. Elizabeth went upstairs, gathered her belongings, and promptly left the house. Carol remained upstairs, comforting the baby and allowing Eli and Angelina space to process what just happened. All along, Eli stayed by Angelina's side. He allowed her to cry herself out, never letting go of her hands.

Finally, Angelina found the words to finish the rest of her story. "I told them I was raped, and they told me I was overreacting. We were going to be married anyway, so it doesn't matter, is what my dad said. My mom didn't say a thing. I interpreted her complacency as agreement. They still wanted me to go through with the marriage. They said we had to get married, because the guru, said 'our auras were made for each other.' I couldn't believe it. Marriage became to me, at that moment, one big lie. I wanted nothing to do with it. I wanted nothing to do with the ashram, where the words of one man mattered more than my own voice.

"No one defended me. The women avoided eye contact with me when I passed them; maybe I imagined it, but I felt like the men gave me knowing grins. Like they knew a secret—my own most private secret. I had to leave. I had to leave…"

"There, there…" Eli held her face in his hands. "You are so strong, Ang."

"I hitchhiked to San Francisco as soon as I turned eighteen. I was able to stay with the aunt of a friend of mine from the ashram—a former follower of the guru—until I could afford to find my own place. I started teaching yoga anywhere and everywhere that I could. I eventually moved into an apartment with a roommate, Erica, who was also a yoga teacher and several years older than me. She took care of me in the way I wanted my mother to. She knew I was struggling with depression and anxiety, but she never forced me to talk about it. She was just there. She'd make me tea, or even meals when I had no energy to do so myself. She helped me find myself again.

"For the next few years, I swore I would never let a man get close to me. I had no trust, no faith, in the male sex. I became fiercely independent and self-sufficient. I also started studying reiki and became a practitioner. I never lost my commitment to yoga or meditation; I was able to separate the truth and beauty of those practices from the lies I was taught in the ashram."

"What were the lies?"

"That women were to be subservient to men, for one. The guru taught that women were to think of themselves as one half of a spiritual partnership in which they serve God by serving their husbands. We were told that if wives disagreed with their husbands, they were to say, 'You're right, I'm sorry. It is God's will.' By arranging marriages himself, he turned marriage into a matter of obedience to the spiritual teacher. It had nothing to do with love, and everything to do with maintaining control and furthering his agenda."

"Wow…" Eli was shocked at how much of Angelina's past he had been oblivious to. He'd always seen her as so centered and…enlightened. He still felt she was both of those things, but now he could see that there were parts of her past that still needed to be cleared. *I'm not the only imperfect one*, he thought, realizing how ridiculous he had been to believe that she was—or that anyone was. "I'm so glad you got out of there. You are very brave, my love."

"I guess I didn't inherit that from my mother," Eli could hear the resentment in her voice.

"That could be true. But she does love you, you know."

"In her own way, I suppose. But not in the way I've needed her to."

"I…I think she wants to heal the past, just as you probably do."

"Maybe. I mean…it means a lot to me that she came here. But I guess I'm not ready to forgive her just yet."

"You will in time. You need to, you know?"

Angelina sighed deeply. "I know."

The couple embraced in silence for several moments before Angelina asked Eli for some time alone.

"Of course," he kissed her head. "Take all the time you need."

AFTER CHECKING IN on his son and finding him fast asleep in Carol's arms, Eli assured his mother that everything was fine, that Angelina was just tired and needed some time to process the past alone for a bit. He did too, he shared, and told her he was going to take a walk. *God knows I need the fresh air,* he thought.

He felt overcome with confusion; emotions rooted in fear began to form knots in the pit of his stomach. He was worried about Angelina, blown away by what she'd shared, and was feeling an even greater responsibility to be a good father.

"How the hell am I supposed to do this?" he said aloud, kicking a stone into the creek he'd played in as a boy. Standing beneath the white pine tree that had been planted on his first birthday, he felt a gust of wind blow by; his skin crawled. He was aware of a slight drop in temperature and soon after, a bright light caught his eye, drawing his attention to a form taking shape on the other side of the creek.

"Michael?" It had been so long since he'd seen him. "Is that you?"

"Hello, Son."

"Dad?" Eli couldn't believe what he was seeing—who he was seeing.

"You seem troubled."

"Well, yeah. Shit. I'm a father now. Everything has changed…"

"It's a great feeling, isn't it?"

"Yes, of course, but…wait, how are you even here? *Are*

you really here? I'm so tired right now, I don't know what is real or imagined."

"Yes, my son, I am always here. Whether you see me or not."

"But…when we talked last…at least, when I *think* we talked last, you were talking about being reborn…"

"I was *thinking* about being reborn. I had a decision to make. And I made it."

"Which was…?"

"I can do more in spirit form than I can in bodily form at this time."

"So what are you? An angel?"

"You could call me that. I'm a guide—not unlike your friend, Michael."

"You know Michael?"

"Yes, of course. We speak of you often. We contemplate when you need us to step in and when you need to figure things out for yourself."

"So, I guess I look pretty pathetic right now then, huh?"

"Not pathetic, just human."

"Sometimes I think it's the same thing. I mean…I can't believe what Angelina just told me. How cruel we humans can be. How terrible men can be, in particular."

"Understood. But not all men."

"That's what I'm so worried about—I have a son now. How do I know how to raise him in a way that turns him into a *good* man? One that respects women?"

"The same way your mother and I tried to raise you. By example."

It was true. Eli couldn't recall his father even ever raising his voice at his mother. Disagreements were settled compassionately, respectfully. And it was often his father who would come around to say, "You were right. I'm sorry."

"Do I have what it takes, Dad? To raise my son as well as you raised me?"

"You have more than what it takes to raise your son well. You are in a position to raise generations of men, Eli. All by example. The world is watching you, not just the eyes of your baby boy."

"But no pressure, right?" Eli laughed uncomfortably.

"You are never alone, Eli. Whenever you need support, you can find me here. Under this tree," he winked. "And I do hope you return here often, with that beautiful boy of yours."

"I will, Dad," Eli smiled. "We will."

CHAPTER THREE

BEING PRESENT

The next two months on the farm passed quietly. Without Carol's support, Eli and Angelina couldn't imagine being able to meet the needs of their newborn and themselves. They were both used to operating on a lack of sleep due to the demands of their hectic careers, but being woken up by a crying, completely dependent child every few hours was another thing entirely.

For every ounce of energy depleted, however, love gave back twice as much. Their son bewitched them. Gabriel already taught them how deeply they could love; lines blurred between pleasure and pain. At one time, Angelina's breasts ached horribly when she experienced a clogged milk duct, but the pain was soon followed by the near-orgasmic sensation of being able to provide life force to her baby. At other times, Eli and Angelina would lie in bed, Gabriel between them, when the love they felt would oscillate between profound gratitude and fear of anything bad ever happening to their child. Now that they had met him, they couldn't imagine life without him.

Petra Nicoll

Despite the occasional discomfort of breastfeeding, Angelina was in awe of its magic. The extra calories her body craved helped increase her milk supply, replenish her own energy, and even helped her lose baby weight—so long as the additional foods were healthy. Carol served her whole-grain foods, including fresh bread, rice, and oatmeal, leafy greens from her garden, and legumes. She was famous for her lentil chili. Angelina snacked on nuts and seeds when she became hungry between meals. She had always eaten healthy, but she had an extra layer of motivation now. Eli, on the other hand, missed the occasional sweet pastry but was committed to supporting Angelina during this transitional phase her body was going through.

It was during a quiet moment breastfeeding in the nursery that Angelina surprised Eli with a question.

"Eli?"

"Yes?"

"I've been meaning to ask you...the day of Gabriel's birth...did you feel anyone else in the room? A man, I mean?"

"A man?"

"Yes...maybe it's silly. It could have just been the euphoria of birth that made me hallucinate or something, but I felt a man standing in the corner—over there," she gestured to the other side of the nursery. "I felt his presence before I later saw him, briefly after birth."

"Really? Interesting. Maybe it was my father's spirit?" Eli had already told Angelina about his conversation with his father by the creek, shortly after their child's birth. To his relief, she had not responded with any surprise. "Of course, he was there. Our loved ones are always near, even after death. Even when we can't see them," she'd said.

"No, it wasn't your father. That's why I'm asking you about it. I didn't recognize the man. Do you have an uncle or older friend, perhaps, that you were close to?"

"Not particularly. Not that has passed away. What did he look like?"

"He was really…quite attractive," Angelina winked. "But I mean that in a majestic way. He was very tall and had wavy, silver long hair. His eyes were…kind. I wasn't afraid. It was comforting having him there, actually."

Eli started to laugh. "That old bugger!"

"What?" Angelina smiled at his joy.

"I can't believe he showed himself to you, but not me! Of course, he would be there."

"Who was it?"

"He didn't even give me a chance to introduce you. That was Michael."

"Your guide? The infamous Michael?"

"One and the same."

"How special that he was there for Gabriel's birth."

"I'm surprised I didn't consider that he might want to be there," Eli leaned back in his chair, his head resting on a pillow as he became contemplative. "He's very invested in my future…and now Gabriel is a big part of that." Eli realized how, since the birth of his son, he hadn't given much thought to the responsibilities that lay ahead of him. He'd focused on remaining as present as possible with Angelina, their baby, and his mother. But soon, the absence he'd taken from his career would end, and he'd be called upon not only to continue making and performing music but to further expand his business investments.

The value of cryptocurrencies had recently gone down, but he knew it was only a matter of time before they would increase beyond measure. Michael had begun to tell him about a "New World Order" that was well underway; elite individuals with a globalist agenda were conspiring to establish an authoritarian government. The shift would take place within his lifetime if he didn't help stop it—and if he managed to do so, virtual currencies would explode.

"Shit," he sighed under his breath.

"What is it?" Angelina asked.

"Hmm? Oh, nothing. Well…everything, really. I'm going back to work in just two weeks."

"I know."

"I don't know what to expect, honestly. I think our world is going to flip upside down, in more ways than one."

"We will land on our feet. I promise," Angelina comforted. "I believe in you. I believe in us." She reached out for his hand and placed her other hand atop Gabriel's head.

"I love you."

"I love you, too."

LATER THAT NIGHT, the whole world may not have flipped upside down, but life on the farm did. It was Gabriel that alerted the family first. Carol, Eli, and Angelina were so deeply asleep, they hadn't heard the distant sound of tires rolling along the gravel driveway or seen the flash of light that illuminated the walls of the guest bedroom that Eli, Angelina, and Gabriel shared at night. It was the light that shook Gabriel awake.

His cries brought the whole house to attention; Angelina reached for him first.

"*Shhhh…shhh…*baby, what is it?" she cooed softly. Eli sat upright, rubbing his eyes. Just then, another flash of light went off.

"Shit, what was that?" Eli removed the covers and shot towards the window, wearing only his boxers and a t-shirt. "It's the fucking paparazzi!" He quickly drew the curtains shut. "Dammit! They know where we are." In reality, he was surprised it had taken them so long to find them. The community was discreet about where Eli was staying, but someone must have tipped them off—most likely for a hefty fee.

Eli reached for his cell phone. His lead bodyguard, Ron, had been given time off during his career break, but remained on call and ready to deploy a local security team should situations such as this arise in his absence.

It was nearly 3 a.m. when he rang, but Ron picked up immediately.

"Eli? What's up?" his voice was groggy, but alert.

"Ron, it's the fucking media. They're relentless. There's a whole team of them out here. I'm pissed enough to go outside and run them off myself, but I know you don't like it when I do that."

"No, no, don't do that. You never know what their intention is—they may even just be fronting as media. I'll get my guys on it. Stay inside. Make sure the doors are locked and all of your windows and curtains are closed."

Carol was already on it; she'd heard the commotion and had sprung to life, the security of her family first and foremost on her mind.

"Done. Thanks, Ron."

"No problem." Ron hung up, anxious to make the necessary calls.

Within eight minutes, four police cars and a team of five security professionals were at the farm, nine people were arrested for trespassing and their vehicles removed, and the peace and solitude of the farm already felt like a distant memory. The property would now need to be manned 24/7, Eli understood from the start. Their privacy was once again compromised—and worse yet, he had placed his mother and his child's safety at risk.

"Maybe we shouldn't have stayed here so long," he shared with his mother and Angelina as the three of them sat on the living room couch. Gabriel had finally fallen back asleep once all the activity subsided and he'd had another meal. The security guards surrounded the house; they were armed and ready, but Eli doubted there would be any more visitors that night.

"It's not your fault, Eli," Carol responded.

"I can't go anywhere without…all this," he gestured out the window.

"That's just part of the price of having your level of fame—but that fame comes with a platform that can help change the world. I'm proud of you, Eli. You carry that burden with grace."

"Thanks for your support, Mom." Eli put his arm around his mother and leaned his head upon hers. "I'm sorry to bring you all along with me on this ride."

This time Angelina spoke up, "There is no ride I'd rather be on, Eli. I can't think of one more noble."

"Thanks, Ang," Eli squeezed her hand. "I guess we should probably talk about heading out of here early. This will probably be all over the news tomorrow."

"Even with all of those people arrested?" Carol asked.

"Yep. Surely they will already have alerted their colleagues about what happened and where we live. Where you live, Mom. What do you want to do about this?"

Carol played with her fingers nervously. "Well, I don't know. This is a lot to take in." Several moments passed before she shared, "I can't leave the farm."

"And you shouldn't, Mom. Not because of them. We can't give them that power."

"But I'll be honest, I don't feel all that comfortable being here alone."

"You don't have to be alone. We can keep the security team on here after we leave."

"I don't really like the idea of that, either…what makes this place so special is its distance from…the rest of the world."

"The property is large enough that we could install a security gate around the edges. You wouldn't even have to have guards around the house like they are now."

"I don't know…"

"I think you're going to have to do that, Mom. At least get a gate. I'll take care of it."

Carol reluctantly agreed. "Can you stay here? Until the gate is up, I mean?"

Eli had never seen his mother in such a state of fear. "Yes, of course. If that's what you want. If we're here, the place will draw more attention though."

"I know. That's okay. I prefer to have you here. Don't change your plans because of…all this. As you said, that would give these people power."

"Okay. You're right. We will stick with our plan to return to L.A. in another two weeks. Let's get the gate up in the meantime. We'll have to keep the security guards here at least until we leave, though."

"Alright."

"Angelina? Are you okay with that?" Eli was not oblivious to the fact that she was likely feeling extra cautious, now that they had a child.

"Yes, I am. We have to get used to this. People are going to want photos of our baby. We have to figure out how to manage that." She winked and added, "Thankfully, we have help we can call upon." Eli knew who she was referring to.

Two WEEKS LATER, a hired driver pulled into the farmhouse driveway, passing through a security check and a tall, stainless steel swing gate. With regret, Eli and Angelina watched as their luggage was loaded into the vehicle.

"The good ole' days are gone, once again," Carol sighed. There were layers to her comment that Eli knew ran deep. "I will miss you three, more than you can imagine."

Eli wrapped his arm around his mother and kissed her cheek. "We will be back, Mom. We'll do this again sometime...I just need to get Angelina pregnant with another baby," he winked at Angelina, who rolled her eyes.

"I think we've got our hands full with this one, don't you?" She smiled as she rocked Gabriel from side to side in her arms. Then she walked up to Carol, "You have been a lifesaver," she said as she kissed her cheek. Carol reached out and took the baby from her arms.

"Oh...I would do it again in a heartbeat. You have blessed me with this little one."

"You know you are welcome in L.A. anytime, Carol. Please do visit often."

"I will, from time to time. But you know I feel most comfortable here, on the farm." Carol glanced ahead at the new security gate. She knew she could never get used to it. "Or at least, I did."

A pang of guilt encompassed Eli's heart. "I'm sorry, Mom."

"Hey, it's all part of the package. I will get by."

Eli noticed the lines and shadows around his mother's eyes. She was getting older, and it pained him to see. He had already lost his father, and he couldn't bear the thought of his mother leaving the earth one day, too. Especially if he had anything to do with it—he was sure the added stress of the incident with the paparazzi hadn't done her any good.

"I love you, Mom." Eli felt closer to his mother than ever before at that moment. The last three months had brought them together in a new way. He was so grateful for the time they'd had to simply be. It was so special to be able to share the start of their new life as parents with one of his own. *I love you too, Dad*, Eli thought as he glanced at the towering pine tree near the creek. *We'll be back soon.*

With a few tears from all except Gabriel, the young family crawled into the car and rode half an hour to the Eugene airport, where Eli's jet and pilot awaited them. A comfortable, two-hour flight brought them to the Los Angeles airport, where they were whisked away in an obscure sedan and brought, finally, to their home at Carbon Beach.

The contrast between their beachfront property and the farm was immediately apparent; the only similarity seemed to now be the tall gate that surrounded them both. The sound of crashing waves could be heard from their front patio and the warmth of the dry afternoon air caressed their skin. They had missed the ocean, but they knew they would soon miss the abundant green growth of rural Oregon.

Ron was already back on duty; he and the gate security guard, Jake, greeted the family upon arrival.

"Welcome home!" The men maintained a friendly but professional demeanor as they were introduced to Gabriel. They knew their jobs had just become more extensive, as the baby drew further attention from the media. It was now their job to not only protect Eli and Angelina but the couple's most precious treasure.

"I brought some of your mail inside—it's already been vetted," Jake shared.

"Thank you, appreciate it," Eli shook Jake's hand and held open the door for Angelina, who was carrying a sleeping Gabriel in her arms. Jake and Ron helped bring the rest of their luggage inside.

"Oh, wow!" The couple exclaimed together upon entering the foyer. Gifts were stacked high along the walls and vases of flowers filled the majority of counter space in the kitchen.

"You have some admirers," Jake laughed at their reaction. "These aren't even from the fans. Those are all down at the office," he said as he closed the door behind them and headed back to the gate.

The gifts in their home came from colleagues, staff, and industry friends in recognition of Gabriel's birth. In the three months that had passed since he was born, Eli and Angelina hadn't even considered the number of people that would want to congratulate them back in L.A. Family and close friends had sent gifts to the farm, but the abundance before them was representative of the music and film industry cultures—excessive. Nevertheless, they were grateful.

"Alright, we'll let you all get settled. You will find the nursery well-stocked for the baby's needs, and the kitchen full of healthy shit," Ron smiled. "I will be in the security quarters. Call me if you need me."

"Thanks for everything, Ron. Truly." Angelina felt relieved to have all the shopping taken care of. Before the baby, she had wanted to remain as independent as possible but carrying bags of groceries and navigating stores with her newborn did not appeal to her. She felt protective of her child, as well as her time.

"Hey, it wasn't me, it was Eli's assistant. I just let them in," Ron winked and left through the front door.

Angelina and Eli released a collective sigh. "It feels strange to be back, doesn't it?" she asked.

"We'll get used to the new norm," Eli answered. "Tomorrow the nanny will arrive."

"God, that's right. I almost forgot." The couple had hired a young woman, Sara, to take over aspects of the role Carol had played in their lives the past few months.

"And I go back to the studio tomorrow. There's some new material we need to record that we started working on before I left. Then my tour will start back up next week. God, I hate to have to leave you beautiful beings," Eli alternated kisses between Angelina and Gabriel.

"We will miss you, too," Angelina kissed him back. Gabriel started to make little cooing sounds. "Somebody's hungry. I'm going to go check out our updated nursery," Angelina headed toward the stairs.

"I'm going to work on clearing out some of these boxes," Eli responded.

It only took a few minutes of alone time for Eli to start getting caught up in his head. The transition back to "normal" life would not be an easy one, he could already tell. He was ready to get back to work and exercise his creative side again, but he also felt a growing weight to be an outstanding father. He wanted to be present in his son's life; he didn't want to miss any of the special moments and milestones that he knew would only come once. *How am I going to balance this all?* Eli crashed onto the couch, closed his eyes, and leaned his head back.

"You know you will have help, right?"

The voice made Eli jerk upright. He saw Michael before him, sitting casually on a chair across from him, his left leg crossed over his right.

"Jeez, Michael. That was some entrance. Where have you been?"

"I'm always everywhere, Eli. Sometimes you just forget you can call on me, so I have to show up unexpectedly like this."

"Yeah, it seems you've shown up to Angelina, too. Were you at Gabriel's birth?"

"Yes, of course. Do you think I'd miss that?"

"I didn't see you."

"You just weren't looking. You were so absorbed in the moment. As you should always be. That's actually what I came to speak to you about."

"What's that exactly?"

"The importance of being present in your little boy's life."

"Yeah, I know. I was just wondering how I'm going to do that. And help save the world, you know—like you keep telling me I have to do."

"You don't have to think of it that way. The responsibility becomes too overwhelming if so."

"Tell me about it."

"Instead, focus on creating the world you'd like your child to live in. Always keep him at the center of your intentions. By creating the best environment for him, you'll be simultaneously creating the best environment for all."

"Okay…"

"These first seven years of your child's life are the most important, Eli. Ninety-nine percent of a human's life experiences are the result of the programming he or she receives in the first seven years of life. Did you know that?"

"No…but that seems a bit extreme."

"It's the truth. A child under seven has a brain that operates at a lower vibrational frequency than consciousness. This is what makes the minds of children so open to imagination. It also is what makes them more susceptible to messaging.

"If you think about it, children who are born into wealthy families are more likely to become wealthy themselves, because they have been shown what is possible. They know they can dream, and have those dreams come true. They have most likely also been told, over and over again, that they can be anyone they want to be. Even rock stars," Michael grinned.

"Hmm. It's true…I mean, my parents were always telling me I could do anything I set my mind to."

"Yes. Even though your parents didn't have much money, they never limited your beliefs. Many poor people fall into the trap of telling themselves—and their children—repeatedly that life is a struggle. That belief kills creativity. So if we want future generations to live more abundantly—not in poverty—wealth has to be distributed among them. To achieve this, everyone has to believe in themselves. They have to be convinced that life is full of opportunity. I know this won't be hard for you to teach your son."

"No, I mean, of course, we will offer him every opportunity we can."

"He is in a unique position though, because some things other children are able to do freely, he won't be able to do. His privacy will be compromised. During these early years, therefore, his interactions will primarily be held within the home. You will need to protect him from messaging that others may try to instill in him. Hollywood is full of corrupt minds."

"I understand. But what happens if I have to be gone a lot? My tour starts up next week already…"

"Your absence in this way will not make you a bad parent. It is more important that the people who are here are positive influences on him, and that when you are here, you are fully present with him. Limit your distractions when you are at home and pay attention to his calls for connection."

"I will do my best."

"You will be fine. Now, Eli?"

"Yes?"

"I will allow you time to settle into your new routines. But soon, I will be back. We have important business to discuss." Gabriel's cry could be heard upstairs and down the hallway. "Until then, it sounds like someone needs you upstairs. Ta-ta!" Michael disappeared as quietly as he'd arrived. Eli took a few deep breaths, then rose to join Angelina and Gabriel in the nursery. *I will be fine*, Eli repeated to himself. *We will be fine.*

Eli gently knocked on the door of the nursery and cracked it open just enough to sneak in. He looked around at the room's features, surprised by how much more alive the space felt now that an actual baby was in the room. He had insisted on painting the room himself, rather than hiring help. He wanted an intimate connection to the room his child would rest in. He'd chosen a gender-neutral yellow for the bottom half of the walls and added eye-level trim. Above the trim, he had placed decals of dancing animals— elephants, giraffes, lions, and monkeys. From the ceiling fan, he'd hung prisms that would catch the sunlight streaming in from the window and hopefully catch the curiosity of his little one. Like the nursery in Brownsville, plants heavily adorned the windowsill.

In the corner of the room sat Angelina, in a cushioned rocking chair. Gabriel was cradled at her breast.

"He's such a hungry little one," Angelina whispered with a smile.

"He's a growing boy," Eli whispered back. He walked behind the chair and rested his hands on Angelina's shoulders, looking down upon his suckling son. "I can't believe how much he's grown in just three months."

"I know, isn't it crazy? Pretty soon he'll be walking on his own and we'll have to watch his every move."

"Who do you think he's going to be? What little personality do you see emerging?" Eli asked.

"Well, he's feisty, that much I know," Angelina laughed quietly. "I think he's going to be a real go-getter, like his father. He knows what he wants, and he goes for it."

"I see a lot of your spirit in him, too. He's always looking around with curiosity, thinking deeply."

"Don't you wish you could read his mind? Babies are so close to God…they remember what the spirit world is like because it was so recent that they existed in that plane. Who knows what he sees that we don't," Angelina wondered aloud.

Eli thought back to the exchange with the spirit world he'd just had in his studio. He reached his hand down and stroked Gabriel's soft cheek, noticing the little hairs and wrinkles on his skin. He took a deep breath and committed the moment to his memory. *I promise to be this present for you, forever and always, Son.*

CHAPTER FOUR

※

THE ASHRAM

Embarking back on his East Coast tour was just as Eli expected it would be—once again, a mixture of pleasure and pain. The pull at his heartstrings when he left Angelina and Gabriel at home was harrowing; he suspected that whatever hormones mothers had that made them ache to be close to their babies had also afflicted him. With each step he took away from their home, he further questioned if he was making the right choice by going back to work.

My absence will not make me a bad parent. Eli reminded himself of Michael's words. He understood that the work he was doing was for his son, too. The vibration of his music raised consciousness. He had to keep recording and performing. Being back on stage reminded him of that; he felt an energetic shift in his audience every night that compelled him to keep going.

It wasn't just leaving his son that was hard, however. While at the farm, Angelina had revealed a fragility he hadn't seen in her before. He'd had no previous knowledge of the deep-set trauma she'd experienced that had caused her estrangement from her family and the ashram. He'd always thought he was the one that needed to heal and evolve; now, he could see that no human was perfect—even the woman he'd put on a pedestal.

This would be the first time she'd be without family around—Eli or his mother, who had become a second mother to her. Would she be able to handle the demands of their son? Even with support from the nanny? Since returning to L.A., she'd begun having occasional nightmares. He didn't know if they were the result of postpartum hormones or depression, but she'd wake up crying and sweating. He'd hold her until she finally would fall back asleep.

He felt terrible leaving her, but Angelina insisted she'd be fine. "You have to continue following your life's purpose," she'd said. As he took the stage later that night in New York City, he knew in his soul she was right. He felt, in a sense, like he'd come home. When he sang and played music, he felt he was offering the truest expression of his being to the world. Feelings that couldn't be expressed in words came forth in harmonies, melodies, and notes.

And he knew his audience felt it, too. When he stood at the side of the stage before shows, unseen to his fans, he watched them. Agitation, irritability, and stress could be felt in the room. As soon as he stepped out from behind the curtain, the energy in the room shifted profoundly. When he struck the first note on his guitar, tears poured down people's faces. Love shined through their eyes. Couples reached for each other and embraced; friends put their arms around each other and swayed. It was pure, natural magic. *How long can I make this feeling last for them?* He wondered.

He knew his work had to extend beyond his music. He had to create a safer, healthier environment on Earth. When

Petra Nicoll

people are struggling to survive or experiencing physical pain or abuse, it's hard to return to love, he knew. *I have to do my part*, he thought. *For my son. For everyone.* That thought kept him going from New York to Philadelphia, Baltimore, and beyond over the next two weeks, until he was able to fly back home to L.A. and the two greatest loves of his life.

When Eli's car pulled through the gate of his beachfront property, it was after midnight. A dim light was on in the nursery upstairs, which Eli couldn't wait to get to. Angelina had told him she'd wait up for him, despite his insistence that she get some rest. The nanny, Sara, greeted him at the door, her brown hair pulled back in a loose ponytail and her tired eyes revealing her fatigue. She'd been napping on the couch.

"Welcome home, Sir," she said.

"Hi, Sara. Please, just call me Eli."

"Yes, Sir. I mean Eli," she answered shyly. "Angelina and Gabriel are up in the nursery. He's just been fed."

"Thank you, Sara. Please, get some rest. Angelina has told me how helpful you've been. You must be exhausted."

"I am a little tired," Sara admitted. "I'll be in my room. I'll give you all some privacy."

"Please, make yourself at home," Eli was already on his way upstairs as he gestured goodnight to Sara. He had to see his babies.

A strange whimpering could be heard, however, from the top of the stairs; he couldn't tell if it was coming from Gabriel or Angelina. He quietly pushed open the door to the nursery, where he saw Gabriel peacefully sleeping in his cradle and Angelina asleep in the rocking chair beside him.

Her eyes were closed, but he could see them moving rapidly behind their lids. Her fingers twitched in her lap as she let out tiny cries.

"Hey, babe, I'm here, it's okay." Eli gently placed his hands upon hers and kissed the top of her head. She remained asleep, in a deep dream state. He tried again to peacefully wake her.

"Love, shh, shh, it's okay." He squeezed her hands this time, with just enough pressure that she opened her eyes, gasping for air. She looked confused for a moment before she remembered where she was and realized she had been dreaming.

Eli caressed her cheek and kissed her lips. "There, there," he said softly. "I'm home."

"Oh, Eli, hi. When did you get here?" she spoke sleepily.

"Just a few minutes ago. You've been having a nightmare again," Eli said worriedly.

"Was I? I guess I was." Angelina glanced over at Gabriel to make sure he was okay. Upon seeing him asleep with his little chest rising and falling, she released a sigh. "It's been happening more frequently lately."

"Ang, why didn't you tell me? I would have come home earlier."

"Because I didn't want you to worry, and to leave your tour. I'm okay, really. Sara has been great."

"We have to figure out what is going on in that head of yours when you sleep."

"I...I can remember some of my dreams," Angelina looked foggily at the wall.

"You can? What are they about?"

"I'm being pulled apart...literally. My left arm is being dragged in one direction, and my right in another. On one side is my mother, and on the other is…a masculine presence. Maybe my father? Or the guru? Or the boy who raped me. I'm not sure."

"I'm so sorry, love."

"I thought I had made sense of all that already…that my past was my past."

"Trauma runs deep." Eli held her close in an embrace. "How can I help you? What do you need?"

"God, I don't know," Angelina sighed.

"Can I suggest something?" Eli asked cautiously.

"Yes, of course."

"I think it might be helpful to visit the ashram. To see your parents, and to have that complicated conversation about what happened that caused you to leave there—to leave them."

"I don't know if I'm ready for that…"

"Okay. So, when you're ready. But I don't think these nightmares are going to go away until you face them."

"When did you get all wise on me?" Angelina smiled.

"Well, you know I have the best teacher," Eli kissed her nose. "I'll go with you. If you want."

"I would like that." She leaned her forehead against his, feeling the power of their unity. After breathing deeply together, Eli pulled back a few inches, holding her face in his hands and looking longingly into her eyes.

"Now, are you ready for bed?"

Angelina grinned, "I'm ready to go to bed with you any day." Eli kissed Gabriel, careful not to wake him, then picked Angelina up and carried her to their bed.

He undressed her from her nightgown with the delicateness of a master lover; unhurriedly, he made his way along her neck, breast, and thighs with his tongue. This night was about her. He knew how to stimulate her clitoris and her g-spot in the ways she liked best; with the practiced perfection of a man who fantasized every night they were apart as to how he'd pleasure her upon his return, Eli made Angelina's earlier cries of distress turn into cries of bliss. As her fierce protector, passionate lover, and partner in life and parenthood, he wanted nothing more at that moment than to make her experience ecstasy...again, and again, and again.

Eli was in and out of the recording studio in the week that followed, but he was grateful to be able to come home and kiss his baby before bed. Angelina would go back to work herself in a few weeks; filming had been deferred for a documentary about Los Angeles' homeless population that she'd been signed onto before she became pregnant. It was a topic of increasing interest to her; the film would bring to light the realities homeless women face who are raising their children on the streets. Anything she could do to share their stories and build compassion for the people society seemed to turn its back on, she would do.

Before returning to the routine of work—and navigating how to manage her career with a young child—Angelina knew there was another kind of work she needed to focus on. If she was to be the best mother she could be, she had to face her demons head-on. She had to come to terms with her estrangement from her parents, and the community that had raised her.

"I think I'm ready," Angelina shared with Eli one morning at breakfast. Sara was in the nursery changing the baby, allowing the couple to have a quiet meal alone together.

"Are you sure?" Eli understood immediately what she was referring to.

"Yes. I have to, for the sake of our son. I want him to have his grandparents in his life. Plus…I need to release the toxic space the past still holds within me."

Eli reached his hand across the breakfast bar and placed it upon her arm. "I think that's a good decision. Your mother really loves you, you know."

"I know. It's just so hard to believe she would turn her back on me like she did. Her silence was, in effect, acquiescence. As if it was okay, what happened to me."

"Visiting her at the ashram will give her an opportunity to explain how she felt. Maybe she kept what she wanted to say inside."

"For over seven years?"

"You kept a lot inside for that long too, you know."

"That's true. Geez, Eli, you're beginning to sound like a guide yourself. Have you been having more talks with Michael?"

"Maybe," Eli winked.

"Alright. Tomorrow. Let's go to the ashram."

"Do you want to call your parents and tell them you're coming?"

"No, they might not want to see me. It sounds selfish, but I don't want to give them a choice. I need to get to the bottom of what happened."

"Fair enough. Tomorrow then." Eli stood and kissed the top of her head. "I'll make arrangements with the band so that I can go with you."

"Thanks, love. I'll ask Sara to watch Gabriel for a few hours."

"Good idea."

IT WAS ONLY a twenty-five-minute drive to the ashram from

their Carbon Beach home, but the two places felt a world away to Angelina. Even though the building was in a residential neighborhood of L.A., she had grown up sheltered within the confinement of the ashram's rules, including rising each day at 5 a.m.; participating in morning prayer for twenty minutes; meditating and practicing Kundalini yoga twice per day, and committing to a lacto-vegetarian diet. There were many other daily rituals and community gatherings she was expected to attend. As a teenager, she had been able to leave on her own accord, but the brainwashing she later realized she'd undergone since childhood limited her freedom.

After leaving the community, she came to realize that the ashram survived on a system of dependency; individualism was not encouraged. The guru desired predictable, obedient behavior from his followers. He did not want his teachings to be questioned. She had become part of the system; she did not question her parents or the guru until she experienced the community's response to her having been raped. Their collective silence and dismissal of the act berated her; it felt so intrinsically wrong, she had to question everything she'd ever been taught.

Angelina's mind was rife with memories as they pulled over and parked a couple of blocks away from the ashram's front doors. It was a grand entrance, with an elaborate patio out front and an arch over the doorway. She wanted some time to center herself in the car before arriving at the doors she had walked out at the age of eighteen, and never thought she'd walk back through again. She took several deep breaths.

"Are you okay?" Eli asked, his hand upon hers.

"Yes. I am."

"You don't have to do this."

"Yes, I do." Angelina squeezed his hand. "Let's go."

Together, they approached the front door. Outside, a couple of men and one woman, all in turbans, sat at a table on the patio. Angelina did not recognize any of them. *They must be newer recruits*, she thought.

All three of the people stood to greet Angelina and Eli with hands folded in prayer and a slight bow. "Namaste. Can we help you?" One man stood slightly in front of the others and spoke.

"Yes. I am here to visit my parents. I am the daughter of Rajat Singh."

The group exchanged glances. "You must be Guru Amrit?"

Angelina nodded as Eli's face demonstrated a look of confusion. He'd never heard her use that name before.

"Yes, of course. Please, come in." The man opened the door and gestured for them to enter.

They were escorted through a corridor and out onto an expansive courtyard with a beautiful garden. Small, individual white cabins lined each side of the patio. The accommodations appeared simple, but well-kept.

Angelina was immediately uncomfortable. Every glance brought back memories. Not all were bad—she remembered playing games in the courtyard with other children, and some of the adults in the community. She saw the small stage where she'd once sang and played the harmonium; that was where her love of music first began. But the energy in the space felt heavy, constricted. She felt watched.

"Guru Amrit! Is that you?"

Angelina turned to see who called her name. She recognized the woman; she had been a friend of her mother's. But then again, everyone at the ashram was considered family.

"Oh, my, it is you! You have grown!"

"Yes, it is me. I have come to see my parents." Angelina did not reach toward the woman's outstretched arms. She had not come to be embraced back into the community, nor did she have any interest in introducing Eli to any member of the ashram.

The woman allowed her arms to fall back by her sides, her smile fading. "I see. I can bring you to them if you'd like."

"Yes, please," Angelina formally replied, knowing guests needed an escort. Eli was caught off guard by her coldness, but he understood its purpose.

Silently, the three turned a corner and walked to the cabin Angelina had lived in many years before. They were led to a wooden door upon which the woman knocked.

"Namaste," she bowed. "You have visitors," She seemed to understand the family's desire for privacy. She nodded and excused herself, which Angelina appreciated.

The door soon opened, and she found herself looking into the eyes of her father for the first time in years. Her instinct was to hug him—she had missed him—but her memory of some of his vicious words from the past boiled within her.

"Father," she nodded.

"Angelina…you've…" his voice trailed off. Elizabeth soon came to the door. "My daughter, you have come home." Tears welled up in her eyes.

"This is your home, Mother, not mine."

Elizabeth did not wish to argue. She looked at her husband, as if for approval, before inviting the couple in. Judging from her daughter's protective energy, she gauged she did not want to be touched. She nodded at Eli and gave a small, uncomfortable smile.

"What brings you here?" Angelina's father spoke next.

"Father, I want you to meet my partner—Eli."

"Very nice to meet you, Sir," Eli extended his hand. A few awkward moments later, Angelina's father finally offered his hand in return, but not his words.

"He is the father of your grandchild, Dad," she thought he might need a reminder.

"I have no grandchild." Her father's words cut through Angelina's heart like a knife. Elizabeth gasped, her face revealing similar disgust. No one would have predicted what happened next.

"How dare you!" Elizabeth spoke through gritted teeth. "I have a grandchild. And if you refuse him, you lose me."

Never before had Angelina seen her mother stand up to her husband—or any man in the community, for that matter. Silence radiated throughout the room, but violent energy was palpable. The moment wasn't about Angelina or Eli's presence anymore; it was a decision-making point for a marriage that had lasted thirty years.

"If you leave me, the community will disown you. You will have nothing, and no one." Angelina detected a subtle crack in her father's voice; he understood what was at stake for himself and deflected it upon her mother. It was a manipulation technique she had witnessed the guru use himself.

"I want nothing to do with this community if its members deny a mother to support and love her child and grandchild. I have had enough."

"You are a disgrace, woman! Leave my home, then. You are not welcome here." Angelina bore witness to her father's attempt to regain his authority and control. She felt disdain for her father and the pattern she had seen play out countless times throughout her life, but she also felt empathy. She knew he had been a victim, too. The guru and its community had seized upon his vulnerability and need for a sense of belonging. He would have a long journey of healing ahead of him, should he choose to do the work.

Elizabeth went through her dresser drawers and removed a small bag of personal belongings; it was as though she'd prepared for this moment in advance, for who knows how long. She wanted or needed nothing else.

"Come, children," she said to Eli and Angelina. "Let's leave."

WITHOUT A WORD, Eli, Angelina, and Elizabeth walked through the doors of the ashram one last time. As soon as they reached the sidewalk, Elizabeth removed her turban. Thick, strawberry blonde hair cascaded down her back. Angelina had never seen her mother more beautiful. She walked with confidence and conviction, adopting an attitude Angelina was sure she must have held when she was younger—one that Angelina herself had displayed when she left the ashram.

They got into the car, fastened their seatbelts, and Eli began to drive. He had no idea where to go, he just drove. Pure instinct, perhaps, drove him to a place he loved— where he went when he needed clarity of the bigger picture, the bigger purpose of life. Forty minutes up the Angeles Crest Highway, he drove onto a narrow, winding road and pulled over at a turnout near the summit of Mount Wilson. It was a clear day; a view of the downtown skyline could be seen, as well as the ocean, far off into the distance. All three got out of the car and stood to take it all in.

"Thank you, Mom." Angelina finally broke the silence.

Elizabeth placed her arm around Angelina's shoulders. The mother and daughter gazed off into the distance together. "You have nothing to thank me for. I was not there for you when you needed me. I've lost so many years…"

"What happened back then? I need to know…why didn't you say anything?"

"I was scared, Angelina. If I questioned the community's silence—your father's authority—it would mean admitting that the last twenty-some years of my life had been a lie. Everything I had been taught would have to come into question. I wasn't strong enough to face those questions."

"How are you able to face them now?"

"Oh, love. To be honest, I'm not sure if I am. But since the moment you called to say you were having a baby… something changed within me. My most primal, motherly instinct returned. I yearned for you, and for that baby. And I knew it was right, and that anything that kept me from you was…wrong."

Elizabeth turned and looked into her daughter's eyes. "I don't know who I am without your father. But I didn't know who I was without you, either."

"Oh, Mom," Angelina wiped the tears from her eyes. "I didn't know who I was when I left you, either. But do you know what? A lot of the tools I learned at the ashram helped me find myself. I continued my meditation and yoga practices, and I discovered reiki. I began to sing again—remember how I used to love to sing as a little girl? And I found new mentors along the way—ones that didn't tell me I owed them something in return; ones that allowed me to think for myself. There is beauty in how you raised me—and how you lived. And it is possible to hold onto those parts and release the others that no longer serve us. You just took the first step. I'm really proud of you."

"My daughter. When did you become so wise?"

Angelina laughed. "Oh, trust me. I've had a lot of help. And I'm still learning. But do you know who one of my greatest teachers has been?"

Elizabeth smiled. "Who?"

"That guy, right over there," Angelina gestured toward Eli, who had given them several feet of distance. He felt their gaze and came forward to join them.

"Eli," Elizabeth began, "I am sorry you were not welcomed more lovingly into our family. My husband felt threatened by you, although he would never admit to it. As for me...I felt intimidated by your wealth and success. Before I met you, I thought you were just using my daughter; that she was one of many women you hooked up with. But when I visited the farm...and met you and your mother...I saw how much love you both hold for her. I was jealous, to tell you the truth. I wanted that freedom for myself—to make my own choices about who I loved and where I lived. To travel the world, like you do. It reminded me of who I used to be."

"That person is still within you, Mom," Angelina offered. "Why don't you move in with us? You can travel with us, too," Angelina winked.

"She's right, Elizabeth. You would be welcome in our home." Eli offered his encouragement.

"Oh, I don't want to impose on your privacy. You both get enough of that, with your careers. Besides, I couldn't handle your lifestyle...having people around all the time. I'm at an age when I want to live simply, more connected to nature. Like your mother, Carol, I suppose," she chuckled.

"Hey, that's not a bad idea…" Eli's eyes lit up. "Why don't you move in with my mother? She's been lonely…I've been worried about her. I'll have to ask her, of course, but I know she'd be thrilled."

"Really?"

"Yes, really. I'll call her now if you want."

Elizabeth considered the fact that she didn't know what other options she had at the moment—but this one felt right. She had felt so comfortable in Brownsville; nestled in green growth, far from the smog of L.A. She could live quietly, but with the anticipation of visits from her daughter and grandchild.

"Alright, then. If I wouldn't be any burden…"

A few minutes later, it was agreed—Elizabeth would be a welcomed presence at the Brownsville farm. Carol could hardly wait to have company.

"Welcome to the family, Elizabeth," Eli hugged Angelina's mother.

"I've missed you, Mom," Angelina added. The three stood in a tight embrace, the L.A. sunset as a backdrop to the end of one era and the beginning of the next.

CHAPTER FIVE

⸺⊸◦◦⊶⸺

THE GALACTIC FEDERATION

The next two weeks passed with far less drama; Elizabeth stayed with Eli and Angelina at their Carbon Beach home and soaked up time with her grandson while awaiting preparations for her move into Carol's Brownsville home. The nanny was given a welcome break, as Elizabeth took over some of her duties.

Angelina's mother was in awe of the property itself; it was in stark contrast to the modest cabin she had lived in for the past thirty years at the ashram. Nevertheless, it didn't take long for her to enjoy its luxuries. She started each day with a yoga practice on the patio, overlooking the Pacific Ocean. The salty air stuck to her skin as her body heated up, adding to the exotic feel of her environs. Physically and emotionally, she felt a world away from the confined and codependent structure of the ashram.

Elizabeth chuckled at the thought that she had left one gated community for another—and would be behind another security gate in the Brownsville home—but she knew she was always free to come and go as she pleased. *No more making choices simply because they please my husband*, she thought with relief. It was a novel idea for her, and one that she took to with surprising ease. *Why did I wait so long?* She questioned, before reminding herself that everything happens exactly when it's supposed to.

After two weeks, the timing felt right for her to return to a slower pace and new phase of life on the farm. Eli arranged for a driver to chauffer her to Brownsville. He had offered to fly her there, but she preferred traveling by car. "I want to feel the distance stretch behind me, to know just how far I've come," she said. She also wanted to stop and visit the Redwoods in northern California, to wrap her arms around those giant trees and feel just how small her problems were compared to the infinite life that surrounds us and that no matter what, just keeps on growing.

Eli had thought that Angelina would be able to rest easier, now that she'd healed some historical trauma with her mother. For a while, she did. She took comfort in having her mother near, especially at a time when she needed help as a new mother herself. But merely a few days after her mother left, the nightmares returned.

It was Sara that dealt with the first few; Eli was often out playing or rehearsing well past the hour that Angelina now went to bed.

"You're a saint," Angelina told her one night after Sara succeeded in waking her, bringing her water, and rubbing lavender oil behind her ears to calm her. On particularly challenging nights, Sara even ran her a bath with drops of lavender, sandalwood, and rose oils. She often had to calm Gabriel in addition to Angelina, if her night terrors woke him. "I don't know what I'd do without you."

"You would manage, Ang, but I'm happy to be here to

help," Sara answered. "I am worried about you, though. We need to figure out what is causing these dreams."

"I know. I thought it was all the stuff brought up about my past with my parents...I feel so much better about all that now, though, and yet the dreams are getting worse."

"Have you talked to Eli about them?"

"Not since my mom left. I don't want to worry him."

"I think he'd like to know..."

"Yeah, I know. I will tell him tomorrow. Thanks, Sara. Please, try to get some sleep. I'll be fine."

"Okay. Sweet dreams," Sara blew a kiss Angelina's way and closed the bedroom door quietly behind her.

Angelina kept her word, choosing to bring the subject of her nightmares up with Eli the following morning while in the kitchen. It was a Sunday and Eli had a rare day off, as did Sara.

"How is my gorgeous woman today?" Eli came up behind Angelina, wrapped his arms around her, and kissed her neck. He had just woken up, but Angelina had been up for hours.

"Hi, love. A bit tired, actually."

"I can imagine. You've got your hands full with this little one, don't you?" Eli squeezed Gabriel's cheek, who sat strapped to Angelina's chest in a sling.

"I do, but Sara has been a great help. It wasn't Gabriel who kept me up...in fact, I think I kept him up."

"What do you mean?"

"My nightmares have come back, in full force. I don't know what to make of it."

"Oh, Ang. I'm so sorry. When did they start back up again?"

"I've had a few since after my mom left."

"Since a few weeks ago, then? Babe, you know you can share these things with me, even when I'm gone."

"I know. I just don't know what you can do about it."

"Well, maybe I can't do anything beyond what Sara does for you. Except…" Eli had an idea. "Ang?"

"Yes?"

"Would you mind if I ask Michael for help with this? Maybe he knows something we don't." Eli laughed at his words, as he realized that Michael knew *everything* he did not.

"I suppose not if you really think he could help?"

"He always helps me when I ask him to—sometimes even when I don't."

"Okay, then. When you feel it's appropriate, go for it."

"Thank you for your trust," Eli kissed her again, this time holding her face in his hands. "I love you so much." Gabriel giggled in between their embrace. "I love you, too, my little rock star."

"Oh, please, one rock star in this household is all I can handle," Angelina winked.

ELI DIDN'T WASTE any time in calling upon Michael. After breakfast and some cuddle time with Gabriel, he retreated to his studio downstairs and settled into his favorite spot on the sofa couch. Merely the thought of asking for Michael conjured up his physical presence in the armchair across from him.

"Dang, you're getting very good at reading my thoughts," Eli remarked.

"No, *you're* getting very good at manifesting me when you need me," Michael smiled.

"Well…whichever, I'm glad you're here."

"It sounds like you need some help processing Angelina's nightmares?"

"Yes, exactly. See, you're reading my thoughts again…"

"I read everyone's thoughts, Eli. Yours aren't special," Michael teased.

"Thanks for humbling me."

"Anytime. Now, let's get down to business. Why do you think Angelina has these nightmares?"

"Well, she might have her own thoughts on it—which, of course, you can access," Eli teased back, "but at first I thought it was because of her past at the ashram with her parents. Now, though, I think it might be something different. Something bigger."

"I concur. It is about something bigger."

"Wait, do you already know what's causing them? Just tell me then, Michael."

"Well, I can't be sure, but I do have some ideas about it." Michael paused for several moments, causing Eli to get a bit anxious.

"I'm all ears…"

"Actually, you're all stardust."

"Yeah, yeah, can you just get to the point?"

"I am getting to the point, Eli. Listen now, what I'm going to share with you is very important. I'm not joking around here."

"Okay…"

"I've waited for the right moment to tell you who you are, really. Who we all are—and what we are—in the grander scheme of things. I think you are ready. At the very least, Angelina is ready. What I share with you today, you can share with her. It may help you both to understand her nightmare situation."

Michael continued, "As you know, I am not human. You know that I am spirit, but I go beyond that. I am from the Galactic Federation of Light." Eli looked up at him, confused.

"It's sort of like your United Nations, but for the entire Milky Way galaxy, which your planet belongs to. All galaxies, in fact, have Galactic Federations of their own, and each is made up of many thousands of civilizations, or what we call 'Star Nations.'"

"You mean like in Star Trek?"

"Yes—your popular culture has alluded to the Galactic Federation before. Star Trek called it the United Federation of Planets. Now, to qualify for inclusion in these Galactic Federations, a civilization (or Star Nation) must evolve to a certain level of maturity. Earth is part of a Star Nation that has not quite evolved enough to join the Federation. The Star Nation I am from, however, has."

"Okay...umm...which one is that?"

"My Star Nation is Pleiades—it is one of the nearest star clusters to Earth. We are a spiritually advanced, or 'enlightened,' culture aligned to Universal Consciousness, known as the Law of One. Each planet—or member—is a free and sovereign being, with the opportunity to evolve toward a peaceful state of Unity. To reach that state, enough individuals on that planet must have shed their layers of darkness—their inner and outer demons—and ascended to a higher state of consciousness—one that is based upon love and light. When that happens, the collective consciousness of the planet rises, as One. Earth is undergoing this transition now, but it is hitting some stumbling blocks along the way. The darkness is fighting back fiercely because it knows it will someday be defeated."

"So...what is your role in all of this?"

"As you know, I am a spiritual guide. I am here to help facilitate this process on Earth by guiding people like yourself. We have rules to go by, however. We cannot do anything for you, we may only guide you. And we cannot show up to everyone. People must be ready and already seeking our guidance—either consciously or subconsciously. If I appeared before some people, I would scare them, instead of help them."

"Well, yeah, you kinda scared me at first, remember?"

"I do. But I knew you'd come around. You had been asking for me in your sleep."

"Wait, what?"

"Every night, when we go to sleep, we go to the spirit world. This is where your dear Angelina goes in her dreams. You go there, too, but she is tuning into the frequency that allows her to experience this other world physically, even though only her spirit is there."

"I think you've lost me..."

"She is traveling forward in time as if she is living the future in the present. One possible future, to be more accurate. When we astral travel, we can go anywhere. We can travel to physical places we know on this Earth, or we can travel to other planets and dimensions. When Angelina travels, she often visits my star system—Pleiades. We have spoken there, although she does not remember me after she wakes up."

"This all sounds so crazy...you have spoken with Angelina? In another star system? When she's lying in bed next to me?!"

"Precisely. And looking back at Earth, what she has seen from there has not been pretty—there are clouds of darkness in areas that the cabal controls. That is when the night terrors come. She then is woken up, either by another or by herself, before she gets to see an alternative future reality—or before she remembers it if she did experience it in her travels."

"Uhh…what is 'the cabal'? You're throwing out a different language to me here, Michael."

"The word may be new to you, but the concept is not. You are familiar with Gemini."

"Gemini is 'the cabal'? What does that even mean?"

"The word 'cabal' refers to secret societies—and there are many—that work inside our governments with an agenda for world domination. Gemini is one of these. And Eli, their members are not all human; some are alien beings, closer in kin to reptiles. Now, highly evolved beings are aware of these societies and their fear-based agenda and are in a position to disempower them. And we are doing this, but we need more recruits, from the humans actually living here on this planet."

"So, what does Angelina see that terrifies her so much? What is the cabal doing that is really so bad?"

"Ah, where to begin? These societies have dumbed down humanity through the use of media, schools, and religions that suppress free-thinking, and through processed foods and pharmaceuticals. They have divided us by instilling fear—the 9/11 'terrorist attack', for example, was an inside job, you know that, don't you?"

"Uhh…I mean, I've heard that before, but I thought it was just a conspiracy theory?"

"There is more truth to 'conspiracy theories' than you humans allow yourselves to consider. The interesting thing is, 9/11 backfired on the cabal. For those that were paying attention, the attack revealed the darkness that resides within your people's government; it served as the catalyst for revealing the truth."

"So how can I help Angelina? And, I guess, on a larger scale, can the planet even truly be saved from this cabal?"

"Oh yes, absolutely, Eli. Here's the thing—the dark forces fear the light. They fear humans remembering their true power; you must never forget that you are the light. The light is your birthright. You must work to vibrate differently than how the cabal has programmed you to vibrate. You have already begun to do this, with your music. Keep playing with your heart; the frequencies of the heart are among the most powerful in the world. And, Eli, continue to fund new inventions that grant freedom to the people of your planet. Have you heard of Nicola Tesla?"

"Tesla, you mean like, the company?"

"The company was named after the man, so I suppose so. Nicola Tesla was a brilliant engineer who created technologies that, if supported, could have granted everyone on your planet true freedom. These technologies are still available to you; new ones are continuously being dreamed of and invented, but as they are a threat to the ways the cabal maintains wealth and control, many of them are sequestered."

"How so?"

"In many ways; their patents are suppressed, their funding is squashed. Your society makes it very difficult for people to afford to think creatively. Too many are indebted to jobs that drain their life force. As we've previously discussed, humans become slaves to money and must rely on the establishments—governments, banks, etc.—to provide loans, credit cards, and whatnot, while the global elite—the cabal—amasses more and more wealth. But you are not powerless, Eli. You, in particular, hold a great deal of power."

"Yes, I know. We've talked about that many times…"

"That is true. But reminders never hurt. Plus, now you know—your power does not only extend across this planet. You Earth humans have such magnificent potential, to a degree never before seen in the cosmos. We from Pleiades, for one, are in awe of what you may become. You all only need to remember this."

"So, remind me again what all of this has to do with Angelina and her dreams?"

"Angelina has merely forgotten the power that you all have. That there is nothing to fear—once you embrace who you are as individuals, and who you are as a collective. And who are you, Eli? Or rather, *what* are you?"

"Stardust?"

Michael grinned. "Exactly. Humans and your galaxy have about ninety-seven percent of the same kind of atoms as stars. Everything you are and everything in the universe and on Earth originated from stardust—massive explosions in the galaxies caused remnants of stars to float around you and through you, even today. That dust rebuilds your bodies over and again, across many lifetimes. Did you know that the bulk of your bodies are newly created every few years?"

"Seriously?"

"You literally go through a natural, physical rebirth every few years. But, even so, you consist of particles that are as old as the universe! Do you know what this means?"

"Not exactly. You're kind of blowing my mind here."

"It means you have the ability within you to access ancient wisdom. It's literally in your cells. Yet, many of you don't stay quiet and still long enough to notice it, except perhaps while you sleep. And even then, you don't remember what you learn in your dreams."

"So, how can we? Remember our dreams, I mean?"

"I will share a trick with you. First of all, before you go to bed, remind yourself three times that you want to remember your dreams. Then, when you first wake up, if you're lying on one side of the bed, roll slowly to the other side. If you're lying on your back, just roll to the other side so you're lying on your stomach. Keep your head on the pillow the whole time you're rolling over. This will dislodge your brain and help with dream-recall. In this semi-conscious state, review all of the details of your dream you can recall. When you are finished, immediately write down all of those details—for this, I advise keeping a journal and a pen next to your bed."

"Okay, we will try that. But, umm, Michael?"

"Yes?"

"How in the hell am I supposed to explain all this to Angelina?"

Michael threw back his head and laughed. "Oh, trust me. She already knows all of this. She only needs to remember."

CHAPTER SIX

A LONG NIGHT

Michael was right, as usual. Eli and Angelina went to bed together that night and when lying in bed, Eli shared what he'd learned about remembering dreams, and the power and wisdom within themselves, while Angelina nodded along.

"Yes, that is all true. Those are good reminders though. You know, I used to record my dreams every day, back when I was living in San Francisco. I journaled all the time, too. Until I met you…it's funny how we break our routines when we fall in love," Angelina winked. "Thank you," she planted a kiss on his lips. "I will start these tricks tonight and hopefully have something to record in the morning… if Gabriel lets me stay in bed long enough to write them down."

"Sara will be here in the morning. She will help if he starts crying, I am sure."

"Yes, she always does…but sometimes he just wants his mama."

"That's easy to understand…I want his mama too," Eli

grinned and reached for Angelina. Her smile demonstrated her openness to what he was suggesting. Together, they disappeared beneath the covers.

THE COUPLE HAD only been asleep for a few hours when what felt like a jolt of electricity shot through Eli.

"Ahhh!" he screamed. "What the hell was that?!" He sat up and turned toward Angelina. She was still lying down, sweating with a heavy breath.

"I…I felt it, too. I think it came from…*me*…"

"What?" Eli questioned groggily. "What do you mean?"

"My dream…it was so intense…that I think my body actually created electricity…"

"Wait…" Eli reached for the journal and pen Angelina had left beside their bed the night before. "Don't get up. Just dictate to me…tell me everything you remember about your dream."

Angelina kept her eyes closed. "It was…about Gabriel. There was a man…he was following us. I was taking Gabriel for a walk, but he was much older…maybe six years old? We were by the water…on a pier…there was nowhere to go…" Angelina's voice trailed off.

"Okay, good…keep going…what did the man look like?"

"He was tall, white…he had a beard, with some gray in it. His hair was short. He was wearing sunglasses…and…a suit? He looked like a businessman, which was strange, by the beach…"

"Did he talk to you?"

"Yes…well, he was talking to Gabriel…he was asking him to lean over the pier, to see the fish…"

"And did he do it?"

"He was about to…his face lit up, he was so excited about the fish…Wait…There was another man, too…He was behind me, I didn't see him…but I felt him there. When Gabriel was about to run towards the man, the other man distracted me. He tapped me on the shoulder…I was going to turn to look, but then I saw through the businessman's eyes, through his sunglasses…they looked…evil. I ignored the man behind me and I shot forward, grabbing Gabriel…when I touched him, I felt…electricity…this love…so deep…" Tears started welling up in Angelina's eyes. "That's when I woke up...when you woke up."

Eli put the journal and pen down and wrapped his arms around Angelina. "It's okay, it's okay…nothing happened… we are safe. Gabriel is safe…"

"I need to see him," Angelina threw the covers back and went to the nursery room, followed by Eli. Together, they peered over the crib. Miraculously, Gabriel had slept through Eli's scream. His little chest rose and fell calmly; his face wore a peaceful expression.

"Oh, thank God," Angelina was still crying.

"See, he is fine. There, there." Eli massaged her neck and shoulders. "Let's go back to bed." They returned to their bedroom, laid back down, and embraced each other tightly.

"What do you think it means?" Angelina asked.

"I don't know…maybe all parents have similar dreams? I mean, we all fear for the safety of our children, right?"

"Yes, but there was more to this. It was orchestrated… by not just these men…by something bigger…global, maybe even beyond…"

Angelina's words reminded Eli of Michael's lesson. *Something bigger.* "The cabal?" he hadn't meant to say it out loud, but he did.

"Actually…yes, I think so," Angelina answered quietly.

So, what *did* Angelina's dream mean? Was the cabal after small children? Those questions kept Eli awake all night, long after Angelina had fallen back asleep. Finally, at 4 a.m. he snuck quietly out of bed and retreated with his laptop to the guestroom down the hall.

He couldn't believe how easy it was to find information; a quick Google search revealed so much content on the topic, he was surprised he hadn't come across any of it before. Sure, he knew about sex trafficking—someone had attempted to kill him the year before for what he knew about a sex trafficking ring in Bangkok—but he hadn't known how extensive it was, nor how massive child trafficking was, as well. He read:

> *There are an estimated 40 million slaves in the world today—across all ages, genders, and races. About twenty-five percent (10 million) of these are children.*
>
> *With the rise in poverty, gender and ethnic biases, social instability, military conflict, and economic globalization, more people have become vulnerable to the highly lucrative human trafficking trade. Demand for human labor—whether it be sex labor or child menial labor—has increased, thereby catalyzing a need to increase supply…*
>
> *The sex slave industry alone generates billions of dollars annually in profits, with the profit for each slave ranging from $11,000 to $100,000 per year…*
>
> *More than one million children are exploited in the commercial sex trade every year…*
>
> *Child workers, minorities, and migrants are at high risk of extreme exploitation, most working in hazardous*

jobs including sex work, forced street begging, leather tan-
ning, mining, construction and agricultural work...
    These slaves are typically hidden from view, working
in back kitchens, shops, and strawberry fields... They have
no freedom to leave... they are physically and emotionally
abused... traumatized to the point where others have com-
plete control over their minds and their bodies...

Eli had to take a break from reading and gain control
of his emotions. His heart ached for all of those people, the
children in particular. *Who is responsible for all of this?* he
thought with anger, before continuing to read:

    Human trafficking is believed to be one of the fast-
est-growing activities of global criminal organizations.
These wealthy business professionals often get away with
their crimes. Law enforcement efforts are challenging, as
there is no one way to address the variations in trafficking
around the world. Differing cultures, religions, and eco-
nomics—combined with corruption and different systems
of justice—pave the way for a thriving human trade in-
dustry.

Michael's words from a previous conversation came
back to him now: "Some of the biggest names in your films,
your music, your government are part of this ring. In fact,
many of them are the same people who are controlling the
banking system."
    The banking system, Eli thought. *I need to get back into*
investing in cryptocurrencies and other new technologies. This
shit is insane.
    Eli remembered the letter he received from an audience

member at one of his shows the previous year. *Monique. I never did reply to her*, he thought, before realizing she had never left her contact information. *Anyway, she didn't ask for a reply. She asked me to do something about sex trafficking—and now I understand it's not only adult and female-based; all children are vulnerable. But god...what am I supposed to do about it?! This is so much bigger than I thought...*

"You rang?"

"Jesus, Michael!" Eli jumped. "Do you want me to wake Angelina again?!"

Michael laughed from his seat on the bed. "I know, I was a bit preemptive this time, but I could feel you were about to ask for my help."

"Yeah, I guess maybe I was. It's...well, your dream-recall trick worked. Let's start there."

"Ah, yes. I had a feeling it might."

"But here's the thing—Angelina could remember all the details, but she woke up before the trauma was resolved. So now we're left trying to make sense of what the dream meant...hoping that we can take its message and see that we have the power to prevent that event from happening."

"Excellent, that is exactly what you need to do."

"So, what gives? What are we supposed to learn from that dream? I assume you know all about it already since you always seem to know everything..."

"Yes, I did hear about it. And you already started your learning process. I see you've been doing some research for quite a while now."

"Yeah, I have. This human trafficking issue is a beast. I have two questions...one, who is really behind all this? Is it the cabal?"

"The cabal does play their part, yes. But you humans

carry out their agenda without much complaint. The male sex drive is quite uncompromising."

"Alright, so that's one issue, I get that. So is cheap labor—or perhaps I should say cheap commercial products."

"Indeed."

"But my second question is—what the hell am I supposed to do about it?"

"Well, as you know, you need to remember your strength. But also, remember that greater strength comes in numbers. Have you spoken with your investment colleagues recently? The ones you met at Burning Man?"

"Not in a while...I mean, Jeff and I had lunch a few months ago but we didn't talk much business. Our investments are growing again, after a temporary decline."

"And I have a hunch they will continue to grow quite a bit," Michael winked.

"Well, I'll follow your hunch. You do have access to the whole universe's knowledge after all." Eli grinned.

"In any case, my suggestion is to reconnect with your colleagues. You'd be surprised at how aware they are of the human trafficking issue themselves. Most likely, they know people involved in it. But more importantly, if you all pool your wealth and power, you may be able to change some laws."

"Is that the best way to combat this? Through the law? The law doesn't seem to be working..."

"You're right, as it stands, it is not. It is up to you all to examine the current systems and structures that allow human trafficking to happen—including your criminal justice system. The corruption in your governments, police departments, and border control—around the world—are a major cause of these crimes. Have you ever considered getting politically active?"

"Geez, Michael, don't start telling me I should run for president or something."

Michael laughed, "That's not such a bad idea. But it's not what I meant. Your contributions to particular candidates can go a long way. Talk the idea over with your colleagues. Pool your great minds, I am sure you all can come up with something. But before that…"

"Yes?"

"As your popular children's book reads and Samuel L. Jackson so eloquently narrates, 'Go the fuck to sleep.'"

Eli did just that. He returned to bed and laid down beside Angelina. He had rehearsal the next afternoon, but he allowed himself to sleep in later than usual—perhaps better stated, Gabriel allowed him to sleep in later than usual. It was as if their baby knew his parents needed time to rest.

Angelina woke up before Eli, but she cherished the shared time in bed together and indulged in the quiet while lying alongside his sleeping body. She had already heard Sara enter the nursery, so she knew Gabriel was well taken care of. Having had her journal alongside the bed, Angelina had been writing for over two hours before Eli finally woke up.

"Good morning, gorgeous," she tousled his hair lightly and kissed his forehead.

"Mmmm," Eli grunted. Mornings had never been his favorite time of day. He reached his arm across his chest and rested his hand on Angelina's stomach. "Morning," he mumbled. "What time is it?"

"After 10 a.m."

"What? Really? What about the baby?"

"He's fine. He's with Sara. He slept in today, too."

"That's a fucking miracle," Eli chuckled. As enlightened as he may have been becoming, he still talked like a roadie.

Angelina closed her journal and put it on the table beside the bed.

"Did you have any more dreams?" Eli asked.

"Mmm? Oh, no, not after that one."

"You act like it was nothing…You nearly gave me a heart attack."

"Sorry, babe."

"What were you writing about then?"

"You're full of questions for so early in the day," Angelina winked. "But if you must know, I have an idea."

"Give it to me."

"After my dream last night, I felt inspired to write another screenplay."

"Really? That's great, love. What about?"

"Child trafficking."

"No shit? That's wild…I stayed up for hours last night researching all about that…"

"Is that what you were doing?"

"Wait, I thought you were sleeping?"

"I can always sense when you're not in bed. Even when I'm sleeping."

"You're so crazy intuitive."

"Perhaps. But we're also just really connected," Angelina kissed his head again. "Anyway, I can feel my creative energy coming alive again. It feels really good."

"That's great, Ang."

"I can feel how it's fueled by Gabriel now. That dream last night really shook me up. I want to do something to help all those kids."

"Yeah, I had no idea how big the problem is. One million children are exploited in the sex trade every year. *One million.*"

"I knew it was high. Gosh, it's just so sad…And most people don't know much about it. We have to bring more attention to the issue, and film is one of the best ways to do that."

"You know what? You inspire me." Eli raised his body above Angelina's. "In more ways than one." He raised her arms above her head and sensually kissed her neck. "Before we go about saving all the children of the world, can we practice making one more?"

"Alright, but then we have to get out of bed and spend some time with the one we already made," Angelina laughed.

"Deal," Eli gleefully returned to the task at hand.

CHAPTER SEVEN

DIMENSIONS

Michael's dream recall tool proved even more effective than Eli or Angelina could have known. With practice and prompt journaling upon waking up, Angelina was not only able to remember her dreams but to access content for the screenplay she was writing. It felt merely as though she were channeling as her pen scrawled across the paper each morning. She saw the characters vividly in her dreams—she simply had to describe them as she remembered them, and jot down the events that made up their lives.

"I think I'm really onto something with this," Angelina said to Eli one morning while chopping fruit for their breakfast smoothies. "Although in a way I feel a bit guilty— as though I'm not writing it myself. I'm just dictating my dreams."

"Don't be silly, you are writing it—it's coming from a deep state of consciousness within you. Musicians often use their dreams as inspiration for their songs, too. I've done that myself."

"Hmm. I never thought about that."

"By the way, did you notice your nightmares have gone away? Ever since you started writing your screenplay a few weeks ago, you haven't woken me up."

"That's true. I think my subconscious has started to see how 'bad' things that happen can end up being 'good.' You know who is waking us up a lot lately, though?" Angelina winked at Gabriel, who bounced happily in his high chair, his face covered in peach puree.

"This little guy!" Eli danced over to their son, who giggled as Eli tickled his tummy.

"That's right," Angelina smiled. "I actually had an idea this morning."

"Yes?"

"I might be able to get more writing done with additional help. For example, from two doting grandmothers?" she winked.

"Aha! Are you saying a trip to Brownsville is in the cards?"

"I am. What do you think?"

"I think our mothers will be thrilled."

"What does your schedule look like the next couple of weeks?" Angelina never could keep track of her husband's commitments.

"Crazy, as always, but the gigs that I have are on the west coast, so I can easily fly back to the farm after the shows. I have some media interviews as well, but I can video conference into those."

"Do you have any gigs in Oregon? My mother still hasn't seen one of your shows, and I know she'd love to."

"If I don't, I'll arrange one," Eli winked. "That's one of the perks of being a superstar."

Angelina playfully punched his arm. "You're so modest," she teased.

ELI'S INCREDIBLE TEAM arranged all of the details—Sara was given time off, which she used to travel to Hawaii (Eli always insisted that his staff not only be paid during their days off work but that they were treated to a trip of their choice); his private jet was hired to transport Eli, Angelina, and Gabriel to the Eugene airport, and a discreet car hired to bring them to the farm; undercover security detail was arranged for not only the farm but the entire town of Brownsville during the duration of their visit. Finally, a private concert was booked at the McDonald Theater in Eugene.

"Invite all of the kids from my graduating class to the show," Eli told his assistant. "Well, what would have been my graduating class," he corrected himself. Eli never did graduate from high school; he'd been offered his first recording contract at the age of sixteen. Realizing how small his graduating class would have been, he added, "And invite all of the students from Eugene's music academies. I want them to see how far music can take them."

Returning to the farm did feel like coming "home," for both Eli and Angelina. The tranquility there felt more like the environment Angelina had grown up in than the flashiness of Los Angeles. Even Gabriel took to the land, like the descendent of farmers that he was. Now eight months old, "rolling in the hay" outside the old barn provided him with an endless amount of fun. He quickly became skilled at grasping for stones and flowers, as well, which unfortunately he also loved to taste. "Look at my little nature boy!" Eli would exclaim. "*Our* little nature boy," Angelina smiled and corrected him, wiping dirt off Gabriel's face.

What gave the couple equal pleasure as seeing their son close to nature was seeing how close their mothers had become over the last few months. They could have passed for sisters, Angelina thought as they'd pulled into the driveway. Carol and Elizabeth had sat on the front porch rocking chairs, their hair pulled back in ponytails and their shoulders draped in matching, colorful shawls.

"Welcome home!" they had called out in unison.

Angelina was also pleasantly surprised at how calm her mother looked. She even appeared younger; her skin was vibrant and her eyes glowed. Clearly, she had also become quite close to Carol. They shared knowing glances and inside jokes that kept Eli and Angelina on their toes.

Music and art had both become hobbies of Elizabeth's, they realized quickly. She had eagerly brought them to the barn and shown them shelves overflowing with colorful, handmade ceramics. "Many more than I know what to do with!" she had admitted.

After dinner their first night together, Elizabeth brought out her harmonium and encouraged Carol to show them "what she'd been working on."

"Elizabeth!" Carol had complained, shyly. "I'm not ready for an audience yet!"

"You learned harmonium, Mom?" Eli had said, excitedly.

"Careful how you answer, Carol," Angelina interjected. "Next thing you know, he'll be bringing you up on stage!" She shared the story about how Eli had surprised her one night by bringing her on stage during a concert—and how it led to Angelina's involvement in his following album.

"Hey, I like to keep things in the family," Eli winked.

"One day, I imagine you'll want Gabriel to join your

band," Angelina replied. As if on cue, Gabriel started cooing.

"See, he loves the idea!" Eli laughed, while at the same time cringing at the thought of exposing his son to the public eye. *Thankfully, I don't have to face that idea for years yet to come,* he thought.

And so continued the family visit; Angelina got some welcome rest and writing time as Gabriel's grandmothers indulged him, and Eli took advantage of opportunities to relax under the white pine tree in between flights and career commitments. They barely noticed the security detail; they remained primarily along the perimeter of the property, affording the family as much privacy as possible.

On one particular day, while laying stretched out in the grass, delighting in the feel of the dirt against his bare feet, Eli was grateful for that sense of privacy. *I wouldn't want anyone thinking I talk to myself,* he thought. For it was there next to the pine tree, as usual, that his father chose to visit him. But this time, Robert was accompanied by Michael. Playing a joke on Eli, they each morphed out of the tree's trunk until they were standing before him and shouted, "Boo!"

Eli surprised himself that he wasn't scared by their apparitions.

"I think I'm becoming so accustomed to supernatural antics, that your sudden appearances don't even phase me anymore," Eli smiled. "I am, however, surprised to see you both together. And delighted. How are you, Dad?"

"Good, Son. Great, rather. Everything is always great in this dimension. It's the earthly folk who have all the problems," he winked. "How are you, is the question?"

"At the moment, quite good. It's nice to be back on the

farm."

"We've noticed you've been more relaxed since you've been here. That's precisely why we've chosen this moment to visit you, in fact," Michael chimed in.

"To rock me out of my slumber?" Eli chuckled. "You can't ever just let me hang out, can you?" he teased.

"There is room for relaxation, indeed—it's important," Michael continued, "But we've given you a few days for family and self-care, and now we must talk to you about 'planet-care,' if you will. Your mind is clearer now to receive the information we have to share with you."

"Fair enough. My senses do feel pretty sharp now. Lay it on me."

"You have made a wise observation. Let's start there, with your senses. You said you have simply become more accustomed to apparitions and therefore did not fear our appearance, but that was not the case. You have heightened your mental and sensory perception. You laid there, staring at this tree for hours. Other distractions—TV, cellphones, traffic, people, stray thoughts—were not present to disrupt your intake. Without knowing it, you honed your remote viewing skills."

"Remote viewing?"

"Yes. It is a mental skill, first revealed to the general public by the CIA in 1995. It is not a new concept, but it remains foreign to most people living in the third dimension. Remote viewing allows a perceiver to receive visual information from a target otherwise not accessible to normal senses. It is similar to what is more commonly known as extrasensory perception, or ESP. In essence, you 'saw' us coming—not with your eyes, but with your sixth sense—so when we visually appeared before you, it was not a surprise to your subconscious."

"Uh…okay. If you say so…"

"Don't believe me? Let's do a test. Close your eyes, tune into your senses, then tell me what Gabriel is doing at this moment."

Eli took a deep breath and did as Michael told him. "He's sleeping on my mom's lap."

"Very good."

"Michael, that doesn't mean anything. That is what he's been doing practically every day at this time."

"True. I was just using that as a warmup. Now, let's do another. Tell me what is happening at Notre Dame."

"Notre Dame? In Paris? How the heck am I supposed to know, that's like a million miles away!"

"Exactly. But distance doesn't matter—that's why they call it 'remote' viewing. Now, try it. Take your time. See what visions come to mind."

Eli laid back on the grass and closed his eyes. Taking several deep breaths, he turned off any doubt in his mind and remained open to any visions that might appear. It took a few minutes for the first, blurry vision to surface.

"Okay, I'm starting to see something," he kept his eyes closed as he described the scene. "I can see the building—I've been there many times, so I remember how it looks, but I'm noticing other details now. The image is kind of blinding… it's bright. But it's not sunlight…it's a red light. I can feel it now, too. It's hot." Eli began to cough. "It's smoky, too. Actually—I can see clearly now. It's on fire. Notre Dame is on fire!"

"Good, very good. Notre Dame is on fire, Eli," Michael confirmed.

Eli opened his eyes. "Wait, are you serious?"

"Unfortunately, yes, I am. You will hear about it on the news if you decide to turn the TV on, or read about it in the papers tomorrow. But I don't recommend it. What is done is done. This fire was an accident, but you need to focus your attention on fires that are at risk of happening in the future—not just physically, but metaphorically speaking. Your planet is on fire, you know."

"Global warming, you mean?"

"Yes, and a number of other…issues. Many of which we've already discussed in previous conversations. The Amazon rainforest in Brazil is burning in epic proportions as we speak; the lungs of Gaia are collapsing. But I'm not here to talk about all those problems right now. I—we—are here to remind you of how to harness your own power."

"Okay…"

"We have some assignments for you, Eli. One is to continue practicing your remote viewing skills. I want to clarify—it truly is a skill, rather than a psychic phenomenon. All humans have the innate ability to perceive things their traditional senses cannot. One way in which you can practice is to pick a random place on the map—a town square, or address number on a particular street. Ask yourself what is going on there—who lives there, what are they doing? You will be amazed at what you're able to sense."

"Sounds trippy…"

"It is in a way—a mental trip," Michael winked.

"It is one you can take any time, to visit me, Eli." Eli looked at his dad.

"Really? You mean I can come to you, it's not always the other way around?"

"Of course not. And this doesn't only work with celestial beings—you can 'visit' other humans on the Earth as well, no matter where they are at the time. Sure could make all the traveling you do easier on Angelina and Gabriel," Robert winked. "You can even tuck your son into bed when you are on the other side of the planet. Babies are more perceptive than adults; he will be able to feel you, if not see you."

"Wow, this is wild."

"It is more common than you think, even among humans. It is merely a matter of manipulating energy to enter higher dimensions."

"You kinda lost me there, Dad."

"Allow me to explain," Michael stepped in. "Dimensions are not places or locations, they are levels of consciousness that vibrate at a certain frequency—with each dimension vibrating at a higher energetic rate than the one below. You have primarily been living in the third dimension—the '3D' world—as most other humans. At times, however, you have entered the fourth dimension; but we will get to that later. First, let me describe the third dimension."

"Okay," Eli nodded as Michael continued.

"The third dimension does not merely represent the things you see. This tree, the river, your clothes, for example—these are all things that still exist in the fourth dimension and to some degree even in the fifth dimension, they are just not as dense. The third dimension is, in fact, a state of consciousness—one that is very limited. It runs on limited beliefs and rules. For example, humans are raised to believe that bodies are solid, so that becomes your reality. You don't look further than that. But in fact, bodies mostly consist of space. Remember, how we talked about being stardust?"

"Yes…"

"Your bodies consist of energy, right?"

"Right…"

"These tiny particles can be manipulated, as your dad was saying, to allow you to merge with other bodies, or—to walk through walls. Or trees," Michael grinned.

"Wait, I always figured that was some supernatural thing, not available to humans…"

"It is very much available to humans. You just have to enter the fifth dimension to access that ability. If you stay in the third dimension, everything is subject to gravity, physical objects cannot disappear, and you cannot read another person's mind."

"Sounds boring, in comparison," Eli joked.

"That is true. You have no idea how exciting things get in the fifth dimension!" Eli's dad smiled. "But of course, you should only use those abilities with good intentions. Power in the wrong hands can be dangerous."

"Now, in order to reach the fifth dimension, you have to first go through the fourth dimension—the latter acts as a sort of bridge to the highest state of consciousness. As I started to say, you have entered the fourth dimension many times in your life, without knowing it."

"When?"

"During sex, sometimes. While you sleep, in your dreams. Angelina is writing her screenplay from the fourth dimension. You have written songs while in the fourth dimension. Anytime you experience moments of spiritual awakening, intense creativity, or deep heart opening, you are in the fourth dimension. In general, this occurs when you're experiencing joy, love, and gratitude."

"That's cool. So how do I get to the fifth from there?"

"Not so fast. I'm not through describing the fourth—

you cannot skip this very important step."

"Okay, sorry. Go on then."

"When you are in the fourth dimension, you feel clear and quiet on the inside. You even feel lighter—because you are. Your body has become less solid, simply by leaving behind excess baggage, such as unnecessary thoughts or distractions. Time no longer feels linear; you no longer are aware of the past or future, but only the present. You are able to manifest in the fourth dimension, faster than you can in the third. Now—to get to the fifth dimension. You actually have found a tool that can be used to help you get there."

"I have?"

"Yes, with your music. To enter the fifth dimension, you need to vibrate in resonance with it. You are very close to entering it when you play your music in 432 hertz."

"I do feel different at those times…"

"There's a chance you've even entered the fifth dimension at those times, but merely for a split second. What you have to master is learning how to arrive there and stay there."

"How can I do that?"

"First, all mental and emotional baggage has to be left behind. Eliminate guilt, fear, anger, and hostility. Those are all heavy, negative emotions that weigh your mind—and your body—down. Practice keeping your vibration high at all times; let go of old, limiting beliefs. Imagine your potential—imagine the planet's potential! Manifestation in the fifth dimension is instantaneous, so if enough people on the planet manage to make this shift to the fifth dimension and visualize peace, there *will* be peace on Earth."

"Wow! So…how far away are we from that reality, really?"

"Not as far as you might think. More and more souls are waking up. Your father here, for example—Robert, do you want to tell him?"

"Sure," Eli's dad stepped forward. "While I was in human form—the form that you remember and recognized—I learned how to enter the fifth dimension and stay there. That is when I decided that my time in that body was complete. Not everyone who enters the fifth dimension has to leave bodily form, but many do choose to do so—and many more are making that choice now than ever before."

"Does Mom know you could enter the fifth dimension? I mean, could you read her thoughts and everything?"

Robert laughed. "That is a very astute question. Yes, she does know. In fact, she can readily enter the fifth dimension when she wants to, as well. We could read each other's thoughts when we wanted to, but to be honest, why cloud your brain with so much content? We only used that ability to communicate silently to each other when we were around guests."

"So why has she chosen to stay in this three-dimensional world then?"

Robert smiled. "Well, that son of yours might have something to do with it. And perhaps she saw the role she could play in Elizabeth's healing, as well. All in all, though, it's an exciting time to be alive on your planet. I think she wants to see, through human eyes, how these times of chaos unfold."

"So, it's exciting in a good way, or a bad way?" Eli asked.

"A good way," Michael interjected. "We have discussed this before. A new reality is emerging on your planet. It's to be expected that there will be some chaos and confusion during the transition. To enter the fifth dimension, everything that does not serve your ascension has to fall away. This means people will experience marital breakups, career changes, and paradigm shifts. What not everyone understands is that, during these tumultuous times, they can always ask for help from higher dimensional beings. People like us, that scare people when we morph out of trees," he added with a laugh. "No, in all seriousness, we don't even need to appear in this visual state to hear a call for help. We can show up simply as thoughts that enter someone's head."

"I'm beginning to understand how all of this works. Are there any other tools you can give me, to help me access the fifth dimension more easily?"

"Of course. There are many. But one that you might resonate with—literally—is Light and Sound Meditation, also known as 'Surat Shabd Yoga.' It is a spiritual meditative practice based on the concept of inner light and celestial sound. The practice uses the dynamic force of creative energy surrounding the universe in the form of sound vibrations."

"That does sound intriguing. Tell me more."

"Like any form of meditation, it is best done early in the morning and/or before you go to bed at night. It is also important to practice on a consistent basis, and while in a comfortable position. The practice begins with concentration. Close your eyes, relax your body, and let your breathing be natural. Picture a dark screen before you; gradually, that darkness will be replaced by colors and light. Choose a mantra—many people choose OM—to repeat continuously, eliminating interrupting thoughts. Then, place your thumbs in your ears to block out all external noise; slowly, you'll start listening to the inner sound of your soul, until you merge with the celestial sound and divine light. You will even feel your vibration rise. It is powerful stuff."

"Thank you, Michael. Thank you, Dad. I'm really happy you came to visit today."

"It was our pleasure," Robert answered.

"Continue practicing these skills, and you will be surprised at the knowledge and wisdom you acquire," Michael shared. "There will be no mysteries at that point. You will be able to visit anyone, anywhere, simply by going there in your mind. You will even..." Michael's voice trailed off.

"What is it?" Eli asked.

"Well, if you wish to know, you will even be able to see who—or should I say what—tried to kill you at Burning Man."

CHAPTER EIGHT

THE CHOSEN ONE

Eli had become accustomed to Michael disappearing after sharing critical new information, but that didn't make it any easier for him to digest what Michael had just said. *What did he mean by* "what" *tried to kill me at Burning Man?* Eli shook his head in wonder. *And geez, Dad, why did you leave me hanging, too?*

He didn't have much time to cater to his curiosity, however. He had to get ready for a gig that night in Eugene—the one his team had arranged for his high school classmates and local music students. *And for Elizabeth*, he thought. He was excited to introduce her as family publicly.

Michael had become closer to Angelina's mother over the last couple of weeks. Now that she was coming back into her true self, he recognized all the similarities between her and Angelina—and even her and his mother. They were both free-spirited, strong, creative women who loved to dig their hands in the dirt, play music, and build things with their hands.

The barn had become overrun with pottery; broken

pieces were used to create colorful mosaics which now formed a walking path from the barn to the house. Music filled the home; the vibration of the harmonium signaled morning and evening meditations that all of them had engaged in together during their visit, except for when Eli had to be away for a gig. An abundance of fresh, organic meals had graced their kitchen table, cooked with love by Elizabeth, Carol, and Angelina while Eli was given quality time with Gabriel. He loved coming home to Brownsville.

The love he felt for his hometown was further felt later that night when he took the stage at the McDonald Theater in celebration of all those who had supported his musical career, and those who aspired to their own. It humbled him when he stepped on stage in the 1925 building and felt intimately embraced by the crowd, which consisted of older yet familiar faces of his youth.

His eyes caught those of his private music teacher, Mr. Sherrett, who he hadn't seen in over a decade. He saw the members of his first band, The Brownsville Rockers. He chuckled to himself at the lack of creativity in their name. He did a shout-out to everyone he recognized that had played a role in his education and career. Then he smiled and announced, "There are also some extraordinary people backstage that I'd like you to meet. Without them, I would not be here today."

Eli then escorted his mother out to center stage. "First, my mother, Carol." The audience erupted in applause. "It must have taken a lot of patience to raise a boy like me," Eli grinned. "But not once did she falter in her commitment to giving me the best educational opportunities and freedom to follow my dreams. Even when it meant dropping out of high school," Eli added. "There are many pathways to success," he continued. "Education is important, but sometimes the best education happens through life experiences. Sometimes our best teachers aren't our formal teachers. They are people who arrive in our lives, sometimes very unexpectedly—in an almost otherworldly way—that have the most profound impact." Eli's eyes began to brim with tears.

"In addition to my mother, my father, Robert, was a key player in my life. I say *was*, but the truth is he still *is*. I feel him with me every day. I feel him now, with us in this room. The people who love us never disappear. Even after death, they are with us. Especially after death, in fact." Carol leaned her head on her son's shoulder.

"And then there are the beautiful souls who enter our lives when we need them the most and teach us far more than we ever could learn on our own. For me, one of those people is the love of my life and mother of my child. Angelina." Eli motioned for her to join him on stage.

"Ladies and gentlemen, this woman is a saint. Whereas my mother pretty much had to live with me, this woman chooses every day to stay by my side. As you can maybe imagine, my schedule can be grueling and my attention pulled in a million different directions, but she remains my rock, always ready to bring me back to center. And…she gave me the most beautiful gift, our beloved son Gabriel."

"Bring him out!" Members of the audience called out. "Where is he?"

Eli smiled, "I know, I know everyone wants to meet him, but you'll have to wait like everyone else and meet him when he's eighteen—on his own accord." The audience groaned. "Folks, I'm sure those of you with children can understand the desire to protect your child. I assure you, he's safe and sound—and the most adorable little boy on the planet." The crowd laughed along with him.

"But there is one more person I'd like you all to meet. Another new member of my family. Elizabeth?" He winked and gestured to Angelina's mother, who stood at the side of the stage, holding Gabriel. Instinctively, she passed Gabriel over into the arms of Eli's security staff and shyly stepped out onstage. "These three women joining me onstage right now are some of the strongest I've ever known. I am grateful to know my son is growing up with such powerful examples of independent women before him. And, not only are they strong emotionally, physically, and spiritually, they are strong musically."

The audience cheered, anticipating where he would go next.

"Many of you have had the pleasure of hearing Angelina's beautiful voice and harmonium playing on my earlier record, and it is only made richer and sweeter in community. Mom, Elizabeth, and Angelina? Would you all share with the incredible people in this room what love sounds like?"

The excitement in the room was palpable. Everyone knew they were in for a magical moment. The women did not disappoint. Three harmoniums were brought out on stage and all were played in unison, while the voices of the three women rang out in sacred tones. They led the room in the mantra, "Om Namah Shivaya," with every last member of the audience joining in.

When the concert concluded after a ninety-minute set of Eli's hits and material that hadn't even yet been recorded, it was clear to everyone present that healing had taken place in that room—healing that some of them hadn't even known they'd needed.

ONLY TWO DAYS remained of Eli and Angelina's two-week

visit to the farm when some unexpected papers arrived via certified mail, addressed to Elizabeth. Perhaps she shouldn't have been so surprised by the contents, she realized later, but simply the fact that she was receiving any mail at all caught her off guard—she had told no one where she had been living for the past six months.

Nothing could be put past her former guru, however, she knew. He had powerful relationships and an ability to acquire personal information that had always confounded her. No doubt, her husband had gone through him to find her.

She knew what the contents of the letter would be before she finished unfolding it. It had arrived through the Superior Court of California.

Petition for Divorce, she read. Her breath caught for a moment, but then an initial wave of shock was replaced by a noticeable sense of relief. She was alone in her room when she read it. She collapsed onto a chair, but not with a heaviness of heart—rather, with a gravitational pull toward the earth. No longer did she have to carry that burden. She was fully free and more grounded.

He wasn't ready to change, she thought to herself. She knew the letter could only mean one thing—he had met someone else. Surely, in the ashram. *He could never be alone*, she thought. Just then, the sound of Gabriel's laughter interrupted her thoughts. She heard Angelina tickling her grandson in the kitchen. *Rajat is losing out on so much*. But he was walking his path, she knew. And she was so grateful to be walking hers.

Elizabeth shared the news with her daughter later that night, with simply a passing mention. "Let's not make a big deal out of it," she said when she saw the look of concern that spread across Angelina's face. "I am fine." She kissed the top of her daughter's head. "In fact, I am far more than fine. I love it here. I love my new life—and my new family."

"I am happy for you, Mom." Angelina hugged her mother, then motioned for the two of them to join the rest of the family on the front porch. "Let's soak up some fresh air together. The night sky is beautiful."

LEAVING THE FARM was always bittersweet. Angelina would miss the tranquility of the home and the loving family support she felt there. It gave her great joy to see her mother so strong and happy, but she was looking forward to connecting with her friends back in L.A. and also meeting with her agent. She had finished the first draft of her new screenplay while at the farm and she couldn't wait to discuss the storyline with her team.

She had decided to set the story in Calcutta, India. The main character was a four-year-old twin girl who was sold into slavery after her parents were forced to toss a coin between her and her sister, since they could only afford to feed one child. However, the girl managed to escape being sold into the sex trade and lived on the streets until the age of ten, when she was picked up by a group associated with Mother Teresa and relocated to the U.S. for adoption.

That was not the end of her perils, however. She was abused by foster families for another two years until finally finding a family that loved her. The story was heartbreaking, Angelina knew, but she wanted to explore the concept of karmic debt and how difficult it could be to break through it—but how worth it that effort was in the end.

Eli appreciated the break from his strenuous schedule as well, although he felt anxious to focus more on his career and investments. He had arranged a meeting with Jeff and other cryptocurrency buddies to discuss the latest rise in Bitcoin value, in addition to other digital currency investments he'd made over the years. *The total value of my crypto investments must be close to $20 billion!!* The number shocked him. He felt a responsibility to use that money for a higher purpose. He was daydreaming about what causes he could invest in during the flight back to L.A. and the subsequent drive from the airport to their home when his thoughts were interrupted by Angelina.

"Hey babe, what are those?" She pointed out the window.

"Hmm?"

"What are all those things on the light poles? Those small gray boxes weren't there before."

"I don't know…probably just radio devices. Antennas for cell service, or Wi-Fi."

"Yes, but why so many of them? They're not usually so close together."

"When did you get so observant?" Eli teased.

"Since I had our child, I guess," she answered, not in the mood to be playful.

"Okay, if you'd really like to know, I will do some research on it."

"Thank you." Angelina leaned over and kissed Eli as he pulled into their driveway. Their security guard, Jake, had anticipated their arrival and let them through the gate.

"Good afternoon, Sir, Maam."

"Hey, Jake. How many times have I told you, you don't need to be so formal," Eli winked. "Call me Eli."

Jake smiled and waved them through. Sara was already at the house, having arrived that morning to make sure the home was stocked with clean diapers and fresh, pureed food for Gabriel.

"Welcome home!" She called out with her typical, cheerful smile. "Let me see that little one!" She lovingly reached for Gabriel, who returned her smile and wiggled excitedly in her arms.

"Don't get too excited, Gabe, it's nap time," Angelina kissed her son's cheek.

"I'll bring him to the nursery," Sara offered.

"Thank you. I'll join you after we get our things unpacked."

Eli carried their suitcases into the house and up the stairs to their rooms—he insisted on doing some things himself.

"I think I may take a nap, too." Angelina yawned as they each put their clothes away.

"Go for it. I'll retreat to my man cave." Eli grinned. He had some work to do of his own.

"Alright. I'll get Gabe put down and then retreat back here. Wake me in an hour please, if your son doesn't wake me first," she smiled.

Eli kissed his wife tenderly. "Your wish is my command. Rest well." He made his way down to his studio in the basement, excited to practice a remote viewing session. He hadn't had much time to devote to the practice since his father and Michael had visited him and taught him the technique. The little time he did have hadn't produced many visions, either. He hoped being in his own home might help, along with the use of some additional tools.

Down in his studio, Eli opened a drawer in his desk and took out an article that had been in the paper about the poisoning attempt on his life when he wandered outside of the Burning Man festival. The man he recognized as the one who had given him tea with belladonna was in the background of the photo. Blonde, dreadlocks, a smirk on his face. *Where are you now, motherfucker?* Eli thought to himself. The thought that this man had attempted to take his life and render his then-unborn son fatherless pissed him off to no end.

I want to see what you're up to. Eli had been promised by Gemini that he would be protected from the man and whoever had hired him to kill him. So far, they had kept their word, and he'd had no reason to doubt their continued support. But the way Michael had brought the topic up led him to question his trust in them. Was there still cause for concern? He intended to enter a deep meditation and see if he could access visions of where that man was now. Having an image of him should help in the process, he thought.

Eli put on his favorite meditation track—it was one of his own songs, titled "Visions." The music had come to him in a dream and never failed to bring him to the present moment. He sat cross-legged on the edge of a blanket. He laid his hands face-up on his knees, open to receiving. He inhaled and exhaled deeply, rhythmically.

After about twenty minutes, the visions started to come. But they weren't what he expected. Eli thought he would see the man from the photo—the one he recognized as human. Instead, what he saw looked…only half-human. The term *cyborg* came to mind, though he only knew it from science fiction movies. This being had the same face and dreadlocked hair but its limbs were robotic, built purely with technology. He seemed to be made of machine.

The being was pacing back and forth, and only then did Eli notice the bars that surrounded it. He was in a jail of sorts, and he was not happy about it. *Who are you? What are you?* Michael wondered. *Who created you?*

Flashes of light changed the scene that was playing out in Eli's mind. The dark jail was replaced by a bright, colorful image of landscaped grounds at an estate in southern California. *I have been there*, he thought. The artificial waterfall and saltwater ponds made him certain that the property before him was Gemini's headquarters. Seated around the long, mahogany table he had sat at during his visit there were several men—some of whom he recognized as the men he met with who had tried to get him to re-sign the contract he had signed in his previous life as Derek Stryker.

In fact, it was that contract these men were discussing now. Eli's head began to ache with the tension he felt in the room, as though he were there now, in person. He strained to make out what they were saying; he had to train his ears to recognize verbal expressions amid the echoes that rang in his head.

"I don't understand how this could happen," he heard one of the men say. "We've been grooming him since his very first lifetime."

"It doesn't make any sense. We've never lost a soul at this level before."

"He is the only soul at this level. He's the chosen one."

"I see no reason to protect him anymore. He's made it clear he doesn't need us. His wealth is at the brink of reaching $40 billion—without corruption! Imagine! For the first time in human history!"

Eli finally knew they were talking about him. *What do they mean, chosen one?*

The men continued, "And when it does, we are screwed. His contract with us will have terminated. He will have discovered that he has free will. And with his influence, the truth will be revealed to others in our charge. What should we do, esteemed men?"

"There is only one thing *to* do. Release the cyborg. As you know, our colleagues in the ring created and pro-grammed this powerful artificial intelligence to kill. He won't stop until his job is done."

Colleagues in the ring? Is Gemini connected to the sex traf-ficking ring? Release the cyborg! Eli noted that they used the term for the being in jail that had entered his own mind. *Jeez, I really am reading people's minds! And these people want me dead…at the "hands" of artificial intelligence!*

The visions Eli was having faded to black. His thoughts became too active to focus on what was coming to him during his meditation.

Usually, he felt relaxed after meditating. This time, he'd never felt more anxious in his life.

How the hell do I explain this to Angelina? To anyone? Is this even beyond Michael, and all other spirit guides and guardians? How can I save myself—never mind the world?!

Eli had never felt weaker.

CHAPTER NINE

※

VISUALIZATION

Eli felt as though he'd stepped inside a horror film, with himself as the target of the film's monster. He couldn't shake the image of the cyborg he'd just seen; the rage in the being's eyes was beyond human-like, it was programmed madness.

He stood and paced within his studio, wringing his hands through his hair and moaning in distress, *"Fuuuuuuck!"* The room was soundproof, so no one else could hear his wails. Except, it turns out, the otherworldly.

"Breathe, my friend."

"Ahh!" Eli startled at the sound of the voice, even though it came from Michael, who now stood in the corner of the room.

"Michael! What the fuck, man? That whole remote viewing thing you taught me is really great, isn't it? Now I have a clear understanding of how my life is going to end. I'd rather have remained ignorant, thanks a lot. What the hell am I supposed to do now?!"

"Well, screaming is a start."

"You're being really helpful…"

"I'm being serious. You must allow your fear to pass. First, you have to move the combustible and toxic energy that arose from those visions. Go ahead—scream some more. Here," Michael threw a pillow at Eli. "Punch this."

Eli was too frustrated to argue. He tore the pillow apart, as a cloud of feathers filled the room. *"Aaaaaarrrghhh,"* he screamed. At last, he collapsed in a heap in an armchair.

"Good, well done. Now, we can talk." Michael spoke calmly and quietly.

"Was that real, Michael? What I saw? Am I really the target of artificial intelligence, programmed to kill me? Does Gemini really have connections to the sex trafficking ring that is trying to have me killed? What did they mean I'm the chosen one? Why are they so concerned about my contract coming to an end?"

"Relax, Eli. Let's face one question at a time. To begin with, yes, what you saw was real. Remote viewing doesn't lie."

"So, I'm screwed…"

"No, that's not what I'm saying. Let's continue with your questions in order, and then I will address what to do about it."

"Go ahead then…"

"Okay. Yes, you are the target of artificial intelligence programmed to kill you. This was recent news even to me. Technology has advanced so quickly that it can be hard even for us ethereal beings to keep up. The 'man' who tried to kill you outside of Burning Man has the ability to shapeshift. He can appear human-like, or robotic, as he looks in his natural state, or even a combination of both."

"What about Gemini? Are they not really who they say

they are?"

"Yes, I tried to warn you of this previously. They are only to be trusted with their word when it is in their own best interest to keep it. They wanted to keep you alive until your contract was fulfilled—and, if they had their way—you signed another. Now, it is clear to them you have no intention of doing the latter, and that you are close to reaching the net worth they promised you in the last contract—but that you will do so without needing to resort to corruption or even money issued by the Federal Reserve. This scares the shit out of them."

"But why?"

"Because these elite members of government and secret societies depend on the ignorance of the people and their adherence to the current—corrupt—economic system in order to get rich themselves. To understand, all you have to do is read *The Road to Roota* comic book that came out in the 1970s and was published by the Federal Reserve Bank. *The Road to Roota* is a secret message to humanity that there is a group of people in the United States and around the world that are working to remove and destroy the financial banking powers that have secretly controlled all aspects of our lives for hundreds of years.

"The original idea of this group sprang from the minds of some very brilliant people and involved rigging markets with computer programs invented in the 1960s. The truth has been hidden in plain sight, Eli, and it will all come to light very soon. I want you to read *The Road to Roota* so you can understand what is happening. By increasing your net worth so much through cryptocurrencies, you are demonstrating to Gemini that people have free will."

"Okay, but what even is free will in this day and age?"

"It is the ability to think, choose, and act voluntarily. In other words, to create your own lives—despite external conditions that may make it appear otherwise. You do not have to accept what anyone—cyborgs and secret societies included—issue to be your fate, Eli."

"I don't know how to keep a being that looks like that from killing me. And wait a minute—you didn't answer my question about what Gemini's relationship is to the sex trafficking ring?"

"Well, they are one and the same, really. Gemini members participate in these rings themselves. They protect each other, at times, in order to protect themselves. If the media were to learn about one person or entity's involvement in a ring, the cat's out of the bag about the others. They are intrinsically intertwined."

"Why didn't you tell me this before?"

"You needed to discover it for yourself. I can't give you all the answers. I'm here to guide you to the truth, not tell you it."

"Okay, but one last question."

"Yes?"

"What did Gemini mean when they said I'm the 'chosen one'?"

"Oh, Eli. Have you not figured this out for yourself, either?"

"Figured what out?"

"That you have an important role to play on this planet—and beyond. The most important role."

"Which is...?"

"We've discussed this many times over. You are to elevate human consciousness. To heal through your music. And..."

"Yes?"

"Well, maybe we haven't covered everything."

"You're killing me, Michael."

"You're also to help save the human race from an alien invasion. But let's not get carried away with that right now...there is something else I'd like to teach you first."

"You must be joking?"

"Sorry?" Michael feigned confusion.

"An alien invasion? That was a joke, right?"

"I'm afraid not. Perhaps I shouldn't have said that now though. I did not mean to distract you..."

"You can't backtrack from that bomb, Michael."

"Okay, fine, I will tell you just enough for now. But then today's lesson must be taught."

"I'm waiting..."

"Well, again, much of this is recent news to me. Evolution is happening so fast. But what I do know is that many of the world's great leaders aren't really...human. Not entirely, anyway. There is life on other planets, you know?"

"I've always thought it was possible..."

"Well, it is so. And some beings on this Earth that are believed to be of this Earth, are not really so. I could be considered one of these, of course, but I come from the light, rather than the dark. There are extraterrestrial beings that are here merely to bring about darkness on this planet. Members of Gemini, for example."

"Okay if that's true, my role in all of that would be...?"

"First things first, my friend. If you are to fulfill that role anyway, you must learn to manage the pressing situation at hand. Your impending doom, per your visions?"

"Right, that..."

"We must first address your fear. Fear is what your adversaries feed on."

"Umm…wouldn't you fear that thing I saw in jail?"

"In my earlier incarnations, yes, I'm sure I would have. But I have since mastered how to harness that fear through a simple but critical tool called visualization."

"What, like in the law of attraction? What you picture with your mind, manifests in real life? That's never really worked for me."

"That is because you're not doing it properly. Let me explain. Your brain has a system in it called the reticular activating system. It is a network of neurons that allows certain information into your brain and blocks out other information. And guess who programmed that filter? You did! And everyone and everything around you, since your first incarnation. So, you have essentially been trained to fear something that looks like that cyborg—through your movies, your novels, and what have you. You have been conditioned to believe you are weaker than monsters. Don't believe that nonsense, Eli!"

"How can I not believe I'm weaker than that being? It's superhuman!"

"You need to embrace your light, Eli. To do this, you must begin by telling yourself you are stronger. If you believe you are weaker, your reticular activating system will find every single piece of evidence that confirms that belief. You will look at yourself in the mirror and notice the parts of your body that aren't as strong as they could be. You will watch the news and note the destruction in the world that you believe you have no control over.

"Did you ever notice how, when scrolling through social media, your eyes are given so many distractions to choose from—so many ads, so many posts—but the ones that win your attention are the ones you believe in? Your mind loves to read things that you agree with because that confirms your filter. Your social media platforms know this—that is why they track your visits, your clicks, and so forth, so they can feed you more of what you believe in."

"I never thought of it that way…I mean, I rarely have time to spend on social media anyway…" Eli counteracted.

"That's a good thing. But also beside the point. You do read the news, don't you?"

"On occasion, yes."

"And you do use search engines online?"

"Of course."

"So, in this way, you go about your life seeking what confirms your filter. You continue believing what you always did—it takes less energy to stay the same than it does to change your mind about something. And, of course, your brain can only process so much information at a time. If it took in every piece of information before you, it would explode." Michael paused for emphasis before continuing, "So do not agree with the message that you are weak, Eli. Or you will *give up*."

"So how do I change my mind about that? How do I trick myself into believing I can beat a cyborg, for Christ's sake?"

"You used an interesting word there—'trick.' That is, in a way, what you have to do. You have to reprogram your reticular activating system to confirm another belief. Your brain has to seek out evidence that the opposite of what you currently believe is true. And you do this by first visualizing what is not yet real."

"Explain that more…"

"There is a two-step method to the process. First, you

must visualize what you want to be true about yourself. If you want to believe you are powerful, you must picture what that looks like to you—and then you must feel it. Try it with me now, please. Humor me."

"Okay, guide me, though…isn't that what you do?" Eli winked.

"Very clever. Okay, I will guide you. First, close your eyes. Take a deep breath." Michael waited for Eli to respond. "Now, in your mind, come to a specific picture of what it looks like to be all-powerful. What does it look like to not have any fear? Don't answer me, just visualize it. What do you look like, physically? Do you stand a little taller? A little broader? Do you take up more space? Next, think about what it would mean in your own life, to be that strong. If someone—something—approaches you in a confrontational way, would you run from it, or would you stand up and stare it down? Picture yourself defeating this being, in any way you desire. Sit with that for a few minutes. I will wait."

Eli continued to breathe deeply, easing his body further into the chair. Fully relaxed, he allowed the visions to come to mind. Michael could tell simply by watching him what he was thinking; Eli began to sit up taller in the seat, his chin raised a little higher, his feet rooted more firmly to the ground. His expression appeared defiant and focused. A slight smile even graced his lips. His confidence was growing.

"Good, Eli. Now, I'd like you to envision your future. You have defeated your greatest fear. You will yet live a long and fulfilling life. So, what does that life look like to you? What are your grandest dreams? This you may share out loud if you like."

"Okay…I see myself still playing music, in front of millions of people. I see auditoriums and arenas full of highly conscious people. I can feel the joy in the room...we are all one. Loving energy is flowing between and among all of us...it is extending out from the vibration of my guitar, and my voice."

"Very good. You have already intuitively learned that you must not only visualize what you will see, but what you will feel. Imagine every positive emotion that you can think of, and then pause long enough to embrace that feeling in your body. What else do you see? What else do you feel?"

"I see myself sharing my wealth. That all of those people who paid money to be at my concerts are actually re-investing that money into poor communities, through me. I feel grateful that I am able to help improve the lives of others around the world through microloans for women, quality education for their children, and free healthcare for all." Eli's eyes began to well up with tears of gratitude. Michael gave him a few minutes to soak in the feeling before asking, "Anything else you'd like to add?"

Eli slowly inhaled and exhaled through his mouth. "Yes. I can't believe how happy I am with my home life. I have a gorgeous, brilliant wife, and our son is such a character. I see him as a five-year-old now, full of boundless energy. He's so playful...and so smart. And that's not all...I see a little girl in our home now, too. She's a toddler...she has Angelina's dark black hair and my hazel eyes. I love her so much..." Eli wept with the feeling of abundance and joy.

"Beautiful, Eli. Do you know what you are doing with these thoughts? You are training your brain to have a different filter. Your brain doesn't know the difference between something that actually happened to you and the things you imagine that are happening to you. To reiterate—the memories that you just created are just as real to your brain as if they already happened. You have just taken a major step toward reprogramming your reticular activating system. Now, back to your original fear—the more you visualize your strength and your power, the greater your strength becomes. How do you feel now, about the cyborg?"

Eli opened his eyes and had to take a moment to even remember what Michael's question was about. "To be honest, he was far from my thoughts."

"Good, very good."

"But now that you mention it, he doesn't seem quite so big. Or quite so evil. He's not even real...how could I have been so afraid? He's just a machine. He can't feel emotion... at least not as authentic as the human kind. Not as powerful as love."

"Excellent, Eli. I am very impressed. You are a quick learner. Now, you need to make this a daily practice. Multiple times a day, if possible. Wake up every day and visualize, even for just a few seconds, how you want your day to go. Picture the life you want to lead, because you are leading it, Eli. No one else is in control."

Eli stood, his confidence having made him feel even taller. "I feel like I could climb a mountain right now. Thanks, Michael."

"You're very welcome. But instead of climbing a mountain, perhaps you should just climb the stairs—Angelina had asked you to wake her from her nap about now," Michael winked and disappeared.

CHAPTER TEN

———∞∞∞———

THE FIFTH GENERATION

A few months passed with Angelina, Eli, and Gabriel spending considerable time in L.A. Angelina had finished the first draft of her screenplay while in Brownsville, so she gave herself a reprieve from her professional goals while her team reviewed the manuscript. She focused her attention and energy on Gabriel and began researching different methods of early childhood development. She was feeling particularly drawn to Waldorf schools. Angelina and Eli agreed on the importance of cultivating their son's creative and spiritual side from an early age.

They both knew that Waldorf education has its roots in the spiritual-scientific research of the Austrian scientist and thinker Rudolf Steiner. They had heard about the Waldorf system before, but now they read some of its history. The German nation, defeated in war, was teetering on the brink of economic, social, and political chaos when Steiner spoke to the workers at a cigarette factory in Stuttgart, Germany about the need for social renewal—a new way of organizing society and its political and cultural life.

According to Steiner's philosophy, the human being is a threefold being of spirit, soul, and body whose capacities unfold in three developmental stages on the path to adulthood: early childhood, middle childhood, and adolescence, and were quite fascinated by it. Not only was Steiner an architectural genius and spiritual teacher, but he also was appointed to be the leader of an Esoteric School for Germany and Austria.

Over the years, the school morphed into an incredible system that is taught all over the world and that integrates the arts in all academic disciplines for children from preschool through twelfth grade. Music, dance, theater, writing, legends, and myths are subjects that are not only taught but experienced. They inspire children's intellectual, emotional, physical, and spiritual capacities.

Until Gabriel would be old enough to attend preschool, Angelina and Eli sought to guide him to reach his highest potential in his current incarnation—with the hope that he would take what he learned and use it to be of service to others.

"The first three years of a child's life are unique," Angelina had explained to Eli, who was less familiar with Waldorf education than she was. "Children are completely open and trustful towards the world. We, the adults, have the responsibility to be good role models because the child's main way of learning is through imitation. Therefore, it's important that we exhibit an attitude of trust, openness, and gratitude toward our son and towards life. Encounters with Gabriel should be respectful, calm, and caring."

She continued, "Through establishing a conscious daily rhythm, we can guide Gabriel into a life based on authentic work. It's important for our son to see us engaging in simple chores such as cleaning, gardening, and cooking and to have Gabriel help us with these, as soon as he is able. From an early age, children make observations about the quality and quantity of sleep we receive, the foods we eat, and exercise and movement we incorporate into our daily lives.

"In addition, Gabriel will need plenty of time to explore the outer world—opportunities to engage with other babies, children, adults, and nature. Along the way, he will develop all of his senses—especially touch, movement, and balance.

"I can see now that this routine could be a little bit tricky to maintain, especially if we are on tour with you. But most importantly, we should try not to be anxious and know that we're doing the best we can with the circumstances we have. I've seen parents that drive themselves absolutely crazy by trying to do everything perfectly and stress out the child even more. I don't want that to be us."

And with that intention in mind, Eli and Angelina went about trying to expose their young son to many elements of life and nature—sand, rocks, dirt, forests, lakes, and saltwater. They arranged times for him to play with other children using toys made of natural materials. Yet, they continued to limit his exposure to the media and the public. As a result, he ended up spending a lot of time in their own home and yard.

They also limited Gabriel's time around technology. Especially in the entertainment industry, among parents with highly demanding careers, Eli and Angelina were shocked to see how much their colleagues relied on smartphones and iPads to entertain their children—even babies!

"No TV even, for this kiddo," Angelina said to Eli one night while stroking their son's blonde hair. They had just returned from a benefit dinner to raise money for homeless youth in the city. Angelina couldn't help but wonder how many of the children they were helping sponsor through the organization had been given technology as a substitute for time and love.

"He doesn't even know what he's missing," Eli added. "Do you, little one?" Eli reached down and tickled Gabriel's tummy. Gabriel typically giggled with the act, but on this occasion, he barely reacted. "What's the matter, Gabe? Aren't you feeling well?" As if on cue, Gabriel vomited.

Eli reached for a spit-up rag. "Whoa! I guess you're not. Sorry, my love. What's wrong?"

"Let me take a look," Angelina reached for the baby. "Did you not like the food Sara gave you at dinner tonight?"

"I guess not," Eli answered for him. "Must have been the broccoli. Don't worry, little guy, I've never liked broccoli myself."

"I better put him to bed. I'm sure that if Sara had noticed anything unusual while watching Gabe tonight, she would have told us. I don't think he's caught a bug, but I'll watch him closely tomorrow after he's gotten some rest. To tell the truth, I'm pretty worn out myself from all that mingling. I think I'll go to bed just after I put him to bed."

"Sounds good, babe. I'm going to spend some time in the studio yet tonight. Remember, I've got a gig here in town tomorrow night at the Coliseum. Are you planning to come?"

"Oh, gosh, that's right. I'm sorry, I forgot about it. I swear, my memory is getting worse and worse these days. I invited some girlfriends over tomorrow evening. Before you get jealous, it's not exactly going to be a 'girls' night'— they're bringing their kiddos. I feel I should keep the date more for Gabe than myself though. Since we were out to-night, I want to spend some quality time with him tomor-row and give him some time with other little ones."

"No worries. You'll only miss the concert of the centu-ry," Eli joked, planting a kiss on her lips.

"Raincheck?" Angelina grinned and kissed him back.

ELI WAS SPENDING less time on remote viewing these days and more on visualization. He fit a few minutes of the lat-ter in that night before his plan to experiment with a new riff he wanted to try out at his concert the following night. Overall, he'd been feeling more empowered since develop-ing a regular practice of visualizing his own strength and picturing the life he sought to lead.

During that night's session, he felt a new sensation—a vibration, or buzzing of sorts, in his internal organs. "That's strange," he said aloud to himself. He brushed the feeling off, attributing it to the movement of energy generated during his meditation.

He was only able to practice about fifteen minutes, how-ever, before becoming overwhelmed with fatigue. "Dang, I guess the benefit tonight did a number on me, as well." Eli placed his guitar back on its stand and dimmed the lights, making his way up two floors to the bedroom. Angelina was already deeply asleep by the time he crawled under the covers. She slept through the whole night, in fact, which he could attest to because he, despite his fatigue, laid awake the majority of the night, tossing and turning.

Eli watched each hour on the clock go by; by the time the alarm went off at 7 a.m., he estimated he'd gotten about forty-five minutes of sleep. "Shit. Going to be a rough day," he thought as he eventually threw the covers off his body.

He could hear Angelina in the nursery, and he slowly made his way there.

"Well, look at you. Long night last night?" Angelina was nursing the baby in a rocking chair by the window.

"Something like that. I went to bed not long after you, but I couldn't sleep."

"Oh, no! What's wrong? Are you worried about something?"

"I don't think so…I don't know…maybe the baby. How is Gabe?"

"He seems fine. No more vomiting. He does seem extra tired today though. Maybe he's fighting a little bug."

"Poor guy."

"Poor you. You've got a gig tonight. You gonna make it?"

"Well, I've certainly performed on no sleep before. I'll go make some green tea. That might help wake me up."

"Good idea. Can you take a nap this afternoon?"

"I wish I could, but I have rehearsal with the guys…I want to play a new song tonight."

"Honey, go back to bed now then. No offense, but you look terrible."

"I have a meeting with my publicist this morning. Didn't I tell you?"

"Um, you may have. Honestly, I don't seem to be able to retain much of my short-term memory lately."

"How could you forget this meeting though? There's been buzz that I may be on the cover of *Rolling Stone* magazine in the coming months…that's what my publicist wants to talk to me about."

"Oh, that does sound familiar. Sorry, love. I must have 'baby brain.'"

"That's strange because you weren't so forgetful when Gabe was first born."

"Maybe I'm just getting old then," Angelina smiled, but seemed slightly irritated by Eli's persistence.

Eli, having become more intuitive lately, replied, "Sorry, babe. I'm just tired. You know I get cranky when I'm tired."

"Yes, I know. It's okay. Just take care of yourself, okay? You really don't look well."

"I will. I'll rest tomorrow. I just need to get through today."

He did get through the day—but just barely. He let his publicist, April, do most of the talking during their meeting. She coached him on the types of topics she recommended he address and the answers he should give to anticipated questions, should she be able to confirm the article with *Rolling Stone*. He always took these suggestions with a grain of salt; she knew as well as he that Eli would say what felt right to say in the moment, suggestions be damned. But Eli knew she was just doing her job, which was to try to protect his brand—for he was a "brand," whether he liked it or not.

By the time rehearsal with the band began later that afternoon, Eli had a pounding headache. He chalked it up to not having slept but given how unusual it was for him to get headaches, he couldn't help but wonder if he was getting sick.

"You alright, dude?" his bass player, Jimbo, asked when Eli began to play out of rhythm. He'd never seen Eli exhibit anything but precise professionalism, whether in rehearsal or on stage.

"Not really, man, I can't hear the beat with all the pounding in my head. It's like I have my own personal met-ronome, that's not in tune with yours. Sorry, guys."

"Are you going to be able to play tonight?" Jimbo looked concerned.

"Yeah, yeah, of course. When have you ever known me to not be able to play when it matters? I feed off the audience's energy when I'm on stage. I'll be fine."

"Alright, dude. Just checking." Jimbo backed off after feeling Eli's resistance to wanting to admit the potential severity of his condition.

"The show must go on" was not just a saying in the entertainment industry, it was a mantra by which performers lived. *I can do this*, Eli thought. He had allowed himself to disappoint fans and his team before by canceling gigs, but he knew this show was local—he could return to his own bed after it was through. *I can make it.*

The show that night started out predictably enough. The band launched into a single off the new record called "Midnight Sun" before Eli joined and played lead guitar for the final chorus. The audience went wild when he took the stage, as always. With so much applause, they probably couldn't even hear that Eli's riff was slightly off. And with the lights so dim, they likely didn't notice how pale Eli looked.

It was when Eli began to sing on the second song of the night that a murmur among the audience began. "Did he just change the words?" Eli heard a lady in the front row turn and ask her friend. He tried to focus on their faces— were they just apparitions? Was this just a dream, or had he really forgotten the words to his own song?

He was aware of his band repeating the last verse at least three times, waiting for him to join back in, but he couldn't remember where he had left off. He looked from one band member to the next, and finally his manager, who stood off to the side of the stage. All of them wore concerned and confused looks on their faces. This had never happened before.

Eli's anxiety built along with theirs, but he couldn't give it much thought; a wave of dizziness washed over him. He clung to the microphone stand to try to maintain balance, but the stand itself fell over; he grasped for something else to hold onto but found nothing. His knees gave way and he fell to the stage. Security guards, his manager, and various band members rushed to his assistance.

"Call the paramedics!" he heard his manager, Robin, call out. Eli didn't know it, but blood was dripping from his nose in a steady flow. "Please…call…Angelina," Eli managed to mutter. *Is this it? Is this how this life is going to end?* He wondered. He felt nauseous enough to die.

It was two days later when he returned to consciousness in the hospital. The experience felt eerily familiar to the time he'd passed out from belladonna poisoning and been rushed to the hospital. Angelina sat next to him, only this time she had Gabriel sleeping in her arms.

"Baby? Hi! How are you?" she whispered, as Eli's eyes slowly explored the room.

"At the hospital again? This is beginning to feel like an annual routine for me."

Angelina smiled, grateful for the promise a bit of his humor showed for his health. "Yep, you scared all of us again. I called your mom, but the doctor spoke with her and assured her you were fine, now that you were here."

"What happened? Did I get some kind of nasty flu, or what?"

"It seemed a mystery at first, but they have determined

the condition, although not necessarily the cause. You showed all the signs of electromagnetic radiation poisoning."

"What? What's that supposed to mean?"

"I don't really know. Talk to the doctor. But maybe it's from all the equipment at your show?"

"That would be weird…I mean, I've been playing on stages packed with electronics practically my whole life and that has never happened."

"I'll get the doctor. He can at least tell you what he knows."

But the doctor didn't, in fact, know much. He knew all of the symptoms he exhibited matched with the condition—insomnia, nosebleeds, headaches, nausea, fatigue, dizziness, flu-like symptoms, and so on. But he did not know the root cause of the problem, although, like Angelina, he suspected it was all of the equipment he'd been exposed to over the years.

"You can go home today, but I recommend bed rest for a couple more days. Keep well-hydrated and stay out of your studio and off stage for a while," the doctor had said.

"Thanks, I will."

"And come back here at the slightest sign of a headache again, alright? Don't try to push through it."

"Will do."

His driver came to bring the family home that afternoon, with Eli's bodyguard, Ron, riding along. As they pulled off the highway and got closer to their neighborhood in Malibu, this time it was Eli who noticed the abundance of gray boxes that had gone up on street poles in every direction he looked.

"Babe, look. There are more of those gray boxes up

now."

"Oh, wow. I can't believe I didn't notice that. Hey, you said you were going to look into what those were—did you ever do that?"

"Sorry, I guess I didn't."

"Hey, could that be related to what is going on with your health?"

"I don't know, maybe. But then wouldn't everyone in the neighborhood be sick, too?"

"Who knows, maybe they are..." Angelina said with a smirk.

"Forgive me for interrupting your conversation, but I know what those boxes are," Ron interjected from the front seat.

"You do? Tell us!" Angelina responded.

"Those are 5G towers. Your neighbor had them installed. As you know, he runs a tech company from his home. He paid the city an insane amount of money to approve permits for their installation. It speeds up his internet and therefore productivity."

"What? Well, geez, it was nice of him—and the city—to tell us about it. How did you find that out?" Angelina asked, incredulously.

"Security guards talk to each other. I ran into Roger from next door last week and he told me about it. It's not just this neighborhood, though. The whole city of L.A. is having them put up—and New York and many other major cities around the country and the world. All the billionaires want the fastest available technology, and they're willing to pay for it—sometimes in under-the-table deals. Companies are selling this to average consumers, too though—it just seems that certain neighborhoods, with more wealth, are having more towers put up."

"Shit. Why isn't anyone talking about this?" Eli asked.

"Oh, they are. It's controversial, but money talks."

"I will get to the bottom of this. I promise," Eli kissed Angelina's cheek. They both looked over at their child, who slept in the car seat between them. No words were needed to express how determined they both were to get those towers taken down.

Eli figured that since he had to rest anyway, he might as well make good use of his time. After Angelina helped him get comfortably settled in their bed, he brought out his iPad and started researching 5G. He was amazed at how much information was available and surprised that he hadn't heard much about it before.

He started with the basics. He typed, "What is 5G?" and began reading aloud:

"5G is the 'fifth generation' of mobile communication technology, set to hit the planet full-scale between 2020 and 2025. 5G technology radiates at a higher frequency, allowing the user access to wireless services through their smartphones, laptops, etc. that is 100 times faster than 4G."

Sounds desirable, at a glance, Eli thought and continued reading: "For example, to download a two-hour film using a 3G network, it would take 26 hours; on a 4G network, it would take six minutes. With 5G, it would take only 3.6 seconds."

Holy crap. Sounds like powerful stuff. In other words, sounds too good to be true, Eli pondered and entered, "Health concerns of 5G" into his search engine and read:

"People in communities exposed to the high-density 5G towers have reported health problems such as insomnia, miscarriage, memory problems, and other neurological issues." Angelina's recent forgetfulness came to Eli's mind. "Children are the most vulnerable to 5G's effects and are quick to exhibit symptoms of electromagnetic radiation poisoning including vomiting, flu-like symptoms, tinnitus, dizziness, headaches, and eye pain." *Oh, shit. Is that why Gabriel threw up the other day?* "Some scientists who have studied 5G concluded that its radiation is actually a carcinogen, capable of altering DNA and causing cancer."

Eli returned to the search engine results page and opened another article—this one stated that 5G has been used as a military weapon, due to its effectiveness at scattering crowds. Another article explained the reason so many towers were going up:

"5G cannot travel over long distances, nor through solid objects. Therefore, every three to ten homes will have a 5G cell tower next to it, in public rights-of-way, and trees in between the towers will need to be cut down. In addition, there is a plan to have thousands of satellites in the airspace above us, beaming down 5G to our technological devices— but also through our bodies and our minds. 5G is actually driving rage right into people. Its frequency is able to affect how a population thinks and acts since the human brain runs on a frequency just like 5G."

Eli lifted his eyes from the screen and glanced out the window. In his line of vision was one of the gray boxes his neighbor had paid to have installed on his property.

"Angelina! Come here, quick!"

Angelina heard Eli's call and quickly ran upstairs from the kitchen and flew open the bedroom door.

"What is it, babe? Are you not feeling well? Do you need to go back to the hospital?"

"We need to go back to Brownsville. Now. We have to get out of here."

CHAPTER ELEVEN

———∞∞∞———

THE NIGHT SKY

As erratic as Eli's behavior seemed, Angelina knew enough to trust his words. At his insistence that they vacate their home immediately, she wasted no time in packing a supply bag for Gabriel and loading the baby into their car. Their exit was so swift and unexpected that their typical security detail was evaded.

Eli insisted to Jake that everything was fine and that they be let through the gate. "Tell Ron I'll call him later," he added as they sped away—with Angelina behind the wheel.

When they reached Interstate 5, she finally broke the silence in the car. "So, what's this all about?"

"Those gray boxes you noticed on the street," he answered.

"Yeah? What did you learn about them?"

"I'm certain they're what's making me sick. And who knows what they're doing to you and Gabriel, as well."

"How can you be sure?"

"It's not even classified information...all I had to do was a quick online search. All of my symptoms match—and even some of yours."

"What do you mean, mine?"

"Apparently, it causes short-term memory loss, which you've been struggling with lately. It can also cause flu-like symptoms like Gabriel experienced. It can cause cancer, babe. 5G actually *changes DNA*. And because of the concentration of towers in our neighborhood, I felt we had to get out of there immediately."

"Maybe it's a sign of the times we live in, but I'm not all that surprised by this. I'm glad you made such a quick decision. With you just out of the hospital, you should be nowhere near those towers. What are we going to do about this, though? How are we going to get them taken down? Are we going to have to move?"

"I need to figure that out yet. I need to go somewhere where I can clear my head. Somewhere far away from technology."

"Should we call our mothers and let them know we're coming?"

"Not yet. I'm thinking I'd like to go somewhere even more remote first. To *really* 'get away from it all,' you know?"

"Where did you have in mind?"

"I don't know. How about we just keep driving…and see what place calls to us?"

Angelina laughed. "I love your spontaneity."

"I've been following schedules my whole life. I'm burnt out by it, honestly. Can you even remember the last time I was able to leave the house without a cavalcade following me? Let's just take this time to indulge in being alone…you, me, and Gabriel. All of my commitments this week were canceled anyway, while I'm supposed to be on bed rest."

"Good point."

"Are you okay driving?" Eli asked.

"Yes, for a while."

"Thanks, babe. I can drive after I take a nap. I just need to rest for a bit."

"No problem." Angelina glanced in the rearview mirror. "Looks like Gabriel is already asleep as well. I suggest you get your nap in while you can," she winked.

"Now you're the one with the good point," Eli smiled. "Wake me when you get tired of driving."

"Deal." Angelina sank into the rhythm of the road, delighting in the cool breeze coming in through the sunroof and the blissful feeling of being with two of the people she loved most in life, knowing there was nowhere any of them needed to be.

ANGELINA HAD MADE the drive between Los Angeles and San Francisco many times, back when she was living in the latter and auditioning for acting roles in L.A. She hadn't had much money while working as a yoga teacher, and it was cheaper than flying to just power through the six-hour drive. Therefore, it came as no surprise to her that she didn't tire driving until reaching Sacramento.

They needed gas anyway, so she pulled over at a gas station just off the interstate. Driving over a speed bump woke Eli, who was shocked to find, upon opening his eyes, that it had gotten dark outside.

"What time is it? Where are we?" he asked, running his fingers through his already wild hair.

"Just after 9 p.m. You slept like a baby," Angelina smiled.

"Whoa, seriously? I slept for six hours?!"

"Yep. It must be the medicine they put you on. You needed the rest."

"But what about Gabriel?"

"He's slept most of the way, too. We stopped briefly at a rest stop a few hours ago for me to feed and change him, but he's quite the traveler. He either slept or stared out the window the whole way."

"Wow. That's amazing. You're amazing," Eli leaned over and kissed Angelina as she pulled into a parking spot.

"I like driving. On the highway anyway, not the city. It's good to be out of L.A. But what should we do now? Where are we going to sleep for the night?"

"Well, I just slept, remember?" Eli smiled. "Let's get gas and use the bathroom here, but I can keep driving. It's your turn to sleep."

"Are you sure? How are you feeling?"

"Honestly, very refreshed. Much better than earlier."

"Alright, that's fine with me then."

Eli did feel like a new person. He hadn't been on a road trip with no responsibility on the other end since high school. He was giddy with excitement and anticipation of where the highway might lead them.

"Ready?" he asked Angelina as she crawled into the passenger seat.

"I am," she reclined her seat back until it was nearly flat. "Wake me when we get there. Wherever 'there' is." She yawned and rolled onto her side.

Eli put the car in reverse and slowly backed out of the parking lot. *Here we go!* he thought. Glancing into the mirror, his heart skipped a beat to see his sleeping child. *One day we will embark on a road trip together, and you will be the one driving.* He cherished the moment he was living even greater when he thought about how briefly it would last.

ELI HAD NO plan in mind other than driving in the direction of Brownsville, as he eventually did want to visit his mom at the farm. He was wide awake, so he didn't need the assistance of music to keep him from falling asleep. He used the quiet time while his wife and son slept to write music in his head.

As it was night, he couldn't see much of the landscape they passed through. He could merely see the names of the various towns he'd probably driven by while on various tour buses in the past. Dunnigan...Maxwell...Willows... he knew they were mostly farming communities, and that the land was relatively flat. It wasn't until he passed through Redding that the landscape began to noticeably change. He felt the gain in elevation and had to swallow to clear his ears.

He could only imagine how beautiful the area was; he had always loved the mountains. It happened to be a clear night, and although he couldn't see the mountains, he could see the starry sky. *Ohmigod*, he thought to himself as he resisted the temptation to look through the open sunroof above him. *I have to see this.*

A roadway sign caught his attention—"Mt. Shasta, 60 miles." *Mt. Shasta*, he thought. *The sky must look incredible from there.* Suddenly, he had a destination. He wanted to get as far from city lights as he could, so he knew he had to take a dirt road that probably led to nowhere. He let his intuition guide him. Several miles ahead, he pulled off the highway onto a road that led into the forest. He was glad he'd recently filled the gas tank because he knew that wherever he was about to go was remote.

The road passed through a thick forest of red fir, Douglas fir, sugar pine, and cedar trees. Even though he'd been raised on a farm surrounded by nature, Eli realized he'd become quite a city boy since then—he had to keep his fear in check to avoid turning back around. He considered the possibility of cougars, bears, and who knew what else. Despite a fear of the unknown, he felt increasingly intense energy he couldn't quite identify. But it called to him, *Keep going.*

It was probably another thirty miles before he was certain he'd arrived at the place they were supposed to be. What looked like an abandoned cabin sat high atop a hill overlooking a valley that he couldn't wait to see in daylight. *A fire lookout,* he thought. He'd read about several cabins such as this that were no longer in use but instead offered to wandering souls who came across them. *I found our home for the night,* he smiled.

He pulled over to park, leaving the car's headlights on and pointed in the direction of the cabin.

"Ang, wake up." He gently rested his hand on Angelina's shoulder. "We're here."

Angelina sat up, blinking her eyes. "Where are we?"

"Our cabin in the woods. Let's check it out." He kissed her cheek and opened the car door. He gathered Gabriel from the backseat, who was still soundly asleep. "Can you take him for a minute?" Eli passed the baby to Angelina and retrieved a couple of flashlights from the trunk of the car. "Let's go!"

The cabin may have looked somewhat abandoned from the outside, but it was clear it hadn't been long since it had been inhabited, at least by temporary hikers or other passersby. It was primitive but perfect. There were two beds inside—one full-size and one twin—with mattresses.

"I can get blankets from the car," Eli shared.

Angelina and Eli looked about at the games and books stacked in the corner that travelers had left behind. There was even a journal with comments from people who had stayed in the cabin before. There was no running water or electricity, but Eli knew they had enough bottled water and even some snacks in the car to keep them going until the morning.

"How enchanting!" Angelina exclaimed, still groggy from sleep. "But really, where are we?"

"Near Mt. Shasta."

"Oh, wow. You really found someplace remote," she laughed.

"We're actually less than an hour from the highway. And there are other roads nearby that probably lead to civilization. I took the road less traveled," he winked. "But you haven't even noticed the best part!"

"Show me," Angelina smiled at his youthful enthusiasm.

"Come back outside with me," Eli led her back out the door. "Look up."

"Incredible! I can see Orion. And look—there's Pleiades!" Angelina exclaimed with excitement.

The latter reminded Eli of a conversation he'd had with Michael—it was the star system he was from. *Angelina goes there in her sleep,* he remembered, but didn't say out loud. Instead, he asked, "Isn't it beautiful?"

"Oh, Eli, it's gorgeous. I'm so glad you took us here!" She glanced down at Gabriel, who had just started demonstrating his hunger.

"I didn't know this was where I was taking us, but something called me here, for sure. Do you feel it, too? There's something…sacred about this place."

"Yes, I do. Mt. Shasta is known for its special energy. Native Americans have always felt that the mountain was the sacred center of the universe. They have stories that talk about it being the home of the creator."

"Really? I had no idea."

The couple gazed at the night sky for several minutes in silence. They felt in awe of not just the planet they lived on, but the entire universe. How vast it was!

A chill ran up and down Angelina's spine, reminding her of the cool night air.

"Let's cuddle up inside," she suggested. "I'm getting a bit cold."

"Sure thing. Let me just grab some blankets from the car." Just as Eli turned to walk away, a bright blue light in the distance sprang him to attention.

"Whoa! Did you see that?!"

"See what?" Angelina had already turned toward the cabin.

"A streak of blue light in the sky. What could that have been?"

"Blue? Are you sure?"

"Yes, I'm sure. Let's watch, maybe it will happen again." They didn't have to wait very long. Within a minute, another blue streak of light shot through the sky, this time following a strange path of sorts.

"I saw it that time!" Angelina exclaimed.

"What in the heck was it?!"

"I have no idea. Except…"

"What?"

"Well, this area is known for UFO activity…"

"Do you think it was a UFO?" Eli scratched his head.

"Maybe. Hard to say. But why not? We both believe in life on other planets, right?"

"True…"

"Anyway, I think it's gone now. Let's go inside. I'm tired,

love."

"Okay, to bed it is."

The couple settled into the full-size bed, using a rolled-up sweatshirt for a pillow. Gabriel slept in between them. It didn't take Angelina long to fall asleep, but Eli still felt wide awake. He couldn't quench his curiosity about what they'd just seen in the sky.

I will ask Michael about it tomorrow, he thought. *Or maybe even do a remote viewing session, to find out where whatever caused that light went.* With the self-assurance that he'd find out the answer, he finally allowed himself to rest.

CRISP MOUNTAIN AIR woke Eli and Angelina early in the morning, along with Gabriel's cries for breakfast. Light poured in through the cabin, exposing the couple to the incredible views they hadn't been able to see the night before.

Mt. Shasta itself could be seen in the distance—the volcano towered above them at over 14,000 feet, radiating its voluminous energy. The mountain reminded them of the duality of how small they were, and yet how powerful individuals can be, too, when their energy is harnessed.

The valley before them was abundant in color; wildflowers such as Shasta lily and mountain violet filled the open meadows where trees didn't overshadow them. An array of bird calls complemented the silence in the air and squirrels curiously explored the ground below.

"What a magical place," Angelina said softly while cradling Gabriel at her breast.

Eli stretched his arms overhead. "It is. I may head over to that field and do some sun salutations."

"Go for it," Angelina smiled.

"Eli followed a lightly traveled path from the cabin

that led to a hollow. He tried to find time to do yoga every morning, but sometimes his schedule prevented him from his daily practice. He couldn't think of a more inspirational backdrop than the one in front of him. He settled onto the earth and went through a series of vinyasas. Breathing in the fresh, pure air he said gratitude for how healthy he felt at that moment.

After a long savasana, he rolled over to his side and pushed himself up into a seated, cross-legged position. He felt perfectly balanced and whole. *Now would be a great time to do a remote viewing session,* he realized. He closed his eyes, his hands resting on his knees, and sank into a meditative mental state.

Breathing in deeply through his nose and out through his mouth, he allowed images of the blue light he saw the previous night to emerge in his mind. Narrowing his focus in on the light, his subconscious began to reveal a form in the shape of what he suspected…a flying saucer. *It was a UFO!* he thought incredulously. *Who…or what is operating you?* Eli allowed his attention to move to the interior of the saucer. His visions focused in on a tall human-like figure with whitish-blonde hair that appeared to want to communicate with him.

Good morning, my friend. The words were inaudible, but they registered clearly in Eli's mind as being telepathic messages from this being. *Yes, it is I you saw operating this aircraft through the sky last night. I am Seth. I am from the Galactic Federation. I led you here so you would see my light. I have a very important message for you that I need you to share.*

Yes?

Millions of your people are planning to storm Area 51 to see what goes on there. But they must not do that. It is a very dangerous place for humans.

Area 51? The classified Air Force base in Nevada?

Yes, that is the one. Here, I will show you.

Eli's visions were transported to a dusty, dry desert. Aircraft he had never seen before were parked outside large building facilities. Armed guards surrounded the base.

Why do people want to storm the base?

They believe there are alien beings and spacecraft kept there. The truth is that dark forces in your government are using the base to manipulate mankind through mind control. The base is a testing range for artificial intelligence technology. They are planning to massacre thousands of awakened ones. They are extracting souls and making artificial intelligence clones.

How will they do that?

They use a substance called "black goo" that breaks down the body, leaving the soul vulnerable to extraction. The goo enters the body through nanotechnology. Tiny specks of computer dust are in the air, all over Area 51. The dust is sprayed from aircraft chemtrails. The ones who will go to Area 51 are in great danger. You must warn people!

Okay, but how do I know I can trust you?

You can ask your friend, Michael, about me. He will verify my testimony. There are many star beings from different space programs working now to warn humanity. Do not enter Area 51! Great danger awaits! Now, I must go, Eli. Rather, you must go. A lot of beings from Area 51 are highly advanced and they will pick up on your presence.

Thank you for your message.

Thank you for spreading it—as far as you can, Eli.

Eli opened his eyes, released a deep breath, and solemnly walked toward the cabin.

CHAPTER TWELVE

FULL DISCLOSURE

"What's the matter? You look like you've seen a ghost." Angelina was rocking Gabriel in her arms when Eli walked into the cabin near Mt. Shasta where they'd spent the night.

"Well…in a way, I feel like I have. Only it was stranger than that—I actually saw an alien." Eli recognized how strange those words sounded, coming from his own mouth.

"An alien? Out there in the field? Are you serious?"

"Not in the field, per se. I held a remote viewing session. I wanted to figure out what we saw in the sky last night. Turns out, it was a flying saucer."

"Interesting. Although I'm not surprised. What all did you see? Did you talk to the alien?"

"Yes, I did. Telepathically, of course. It was a male figure, flying the saucer. He said he wanted me to see him, so I could warn other people."

"About what exactly?"

"About what is going on at Area 51—the Air Force base in Nevada."

"What is going on there?"

Eli proceeded to share the entire conversation he'd had with the being, as Angelina listened as attentively as Gabriel would allow.

"Do you think all of that is true? Do you think the government is planning to 'massacre thousands of awakened ones'?" Angelina's eyes grew wide.

"I plan to ask Michael about it, as the being suggested. I feel like he was telling me the truth, but I want to confirm it."

"Things are worse than I thought…" Angelina looked down at their child with a worried expression. "What do you plan to do about all of this? If it is true?"

"Well, he asked me to spread the message. But I need guidance about that, too…"

Angelina looked out across the valley, toward the peak of Mt. Shasta. "Well, this is a beautiful place and I hate to leave it, but I think we should continue to Brownsville. We can rest while we're there. Our moms will be sure to fuss over Gabriel and give us some time to think about next steps."

"That's true. I'm ready to get going. I'm getting hungry for a real meal, too. Let me give my mom a call. If we're lucky, she'll have something fresh from the farm cooked for us by lunchtime."

"And maybe my mom will have one of her marionberry pies made." Angelina laughed, "I guess we're never too old to crave our mothers' cooking."

"Oh! And I should probably call Ron when we have cell reception again. He must be worried about us."

"Good idea. Have him notify the security detail in Brownsville that we're coming, please. I don't want to take any chances with Gabriel."

"Will do," Eli kissed Angelina as they headed toward the car.

While Angelina took her turn driving, Eli called Ron first and was assured there'd be a security team ready at the farm by their arrival. He then called his mother. Both Carol and Elizabeth were thrilled by the news of their unexpected visit. "Bring that little boy of yours to me!" Carol had squealed. She also sensed concern and emotional fatigue in Eli's voice, but she preferred to ask him about it at the right moment after they had arrived on the farm.

Snacks and bottled water tied them over during the drive; they just made one quick stop in Ashland, Oregon for gas and a bathroom break before continuing to the farm. They were welcomed with the joy and elation they were accustomed to receiving from their mothers, but it was Gabriel who received the majority of the initial attention.

"Look how big you're getting!" Elizabeth reached for the baby and began to bounce him on her hip, to Gabriel's delight.

"You must be tired," Carol assessed. "Come, come on inside. You have time to freshen up before lunch is served, and the bed is ready for you both to take a siesta after our meal."

"How can you know exactly the order of my desires?" Eli smiled.

"I've known you my whole life, Son," Carol winked.

After Eli and Angelina took a quick shower—together, which they had always loved to do but hadn't been able to very often since having Gabriel—they settled into dining room chairs around a farm-to-table feast. Being late fall, the garden was abundant with giant zucchini, heirloom tomato, squash blossoms, rainbow carrots, arugula, and so much more. The harvest had been artistically and lovingly transformed into colorful salads and a hearty soup.

After eating so much, Angelina had nearly forgotten about her earlier craving for dessert when her mother came back to the table, carrying a marionberry-rhubarb crisp. "I tried something a little bit different this time. I hope you like it," Elizabeth placed a kiss on her daughter's head as she laid the dish on the table.

"Mom! That looks amazing!"

"It will taste even better, I assure you," Carol smiled. "Angelina, your mother is quite the baker."

"Trust me, I know," Angelina grinned back.

After indulging in a second serving of cobbler, Eli and Angelina retreated to the bedroom for a nap.

"Gabriel is in good hands," Carol had said. "We will leave the cleanup for later—for now, we will indulge in entertaining our grandson. Go get some rest, you two."

An hour of rest recharged the couple, leaving Eli feeling balanced enough to face some of the difficult decisions he knew he had to discuss with Michael.

"I'll go visit with our moms," Angelina offered. "You go take the time you need to process your next steps."

"Thanks, love," Eli kissed Angelina tenderly. "I appreciate you."

"The whole world appreciates you," Angelina kissed him back.

Eli made his way quietly out the back door and toward the creek. He took a seat next to the white pine tree and wasted no time getting straight to the point.

"Michael, I need your help. I've got some serious questions for you."

"You know I'm always here," Michael poked his head out from behind the tree.

"Hey, Michael. Thanks for coming so quickly."

"My pleasure."

"So…you know what brought me here, right?"

"To Brownsville? You made a discovery about 5G—after becoming quite sick, yes?"

"Yes, although that already feels like forever ago. A lot has happened since then even, but let's start there. What the heck can I do about all those 5G towers going up? Not only in my neighborhood, but around the world?"

"You are an influencer, Eli. You know this. And, you know that your music helps heal people. But do you remember that your music actually *changes* DNA? 5G can change DNA and cause cancer, but your music can *change that DNA back*. You could have used that tool on your own body, had you thought to listen to your last album while in the hospital bed. In fact, that is why Angelina and Gabriel didn't get as sick as you—did you know Angelina plays your music in the nursery while she's breastfeeding? And before she puts Gabriel to bed?"

"Yeah, I guess I did. Sometimes, anyway."

"Your music isn't enough to counteract the effects of 5G entirely, however. You must do more. Invest in some quartz crystals—this is an easy way to compound the healing benefits of your music. Crystals absorb energy, so they can remove the harmful frequencies emitted by 5G. Place them around each room of your house and consider buying one massive quartz crystal for the center of your home. It's wonderfully decorative, by the way," Michael smiled.

"I'm concerned about more than décor, Michael."

"Indeed. Just trying to lighten the mood. There is much

more you can do to combat harmful wireless technology, by the way."

"I'm still listening…"

"Well, obviously, don't use smartphones as much. Use landline phones whenever possible. Smartphones have the ability to change your brain, did you know that?"

"I do now."

"But that should be the least of your worries. The human body and brain are being manipulated by much stronger forces. Humans are essentially becoming machines—you already are, in many ways."

"What do you mean by that?"

"I mean that, with the infiltration of technology—the internet, social media, your smartphones and all of the apps you use on them—humans are already one with machines. If all of these tools were to be taken away, it would be hard for most of you to function. Nearly all economic transactions are done online, are they not? Your medical records are kept electronically. Some people are hooked up to machines simply to survive—to breathe, to have a heartbeat. People around the world are willing to have wearable and even injectable electronics. You are close to reaching the point of what is called technological 'singularity,' where artificial intelligence supersedes human intellect. That may spell the end of the human race, as we know it."

"How far away are we from that point? Or should I say how close?" Eli asked.

"Too close for comfort, that's for sure. But this is where you come in, again. As an influencer, you also have a voice much louder than the average person on this planet. Use it, Eli. Speak to your audiences, speak to your politicians. Tell them why you don't want 5G—why *they* don't want 5G.

But beyond that, you must warn the human race about how they're being deceived."

"How are we being deceived?"

"You are being brainwashed to believe that some technological tools—ones that enter and control your bodies—are actually *benefits*. Some injectable devices, for example, are being sold as tools to warn you—and healthcare providers—of illnesses in your body. But make no mistake, Eli. These are devices that will be used against you. Every individual will become but a cog in the machine. One giant, all-powerful machine."

Eli took several deep breaths to digest everything that Michael just shared with him.

"So, Michael?"

"Yes?"

"Is this all connected to what is going on at Area 51?"

"Ah. Yes, the conversation you had during your remote viewing session, right?"

"You know about that?"

"Of course. Seth told me about it. He is from my galaxy, you know."

"So…everything he told me was real?"

"Unfortunately, yes. The goal of elite societies—such as Gemini—is to entrap humans into ongoing servitude. This is done through mind control and control of finance, government, media, and military police. Once humans are microchipped, however, the use of mind control becomes moot. It is a whole different level of manipulation. What is happening at Area 51 is these elite leaders are using human souls to make artificial intelligence clones, which can be programmed to act in accordance with their will. 5G is a steppingstone to human dependence on technology that leads individuals to offer their minds and bodies to dark forces that will eventually extract their souls. Furthermore, Eli, human trafficking is being used as another pathway to extract souls. As you can gather, this is not pretty business."

Eli ran his fingers through his hair and stared into the creek. "I don't even know what to say, Michael. This is huge."

"Yes. I've been trying to warn you about the danger of your times for quite some time now. But I needed to do so gradually, so as not to overwhelm you. I don't think you would have even believed anything I've told you, had I told you all of this at the beginning of our relationship."

"Yeah, that's probably true. But if I wouldn't even have believed you, how can we get mainstream society to believe all this? How am I supposed to warn people?"

"If your popular culture starts to speak of it, that is a start. These themes must enter your music, movies, and books. And your magazines."

Magazines. Eli's eyes lit up. "Like *Rolling Stone?*"

Michael grinned. "For example."

"And...like Angelina's screenplay?"

"That as well. If she so chooses."

"But...doesn't that open us up to a hell of a lot of risks? I mean, people already want me dead for uncovering that sex trafficking ring in Thailand. Aren't they *really* going to want me dead if I share all of this information? And... would they possibly even come after our son? I can't handle that, Michael."

"I would say that you can't handle the alternative. Would you prefer that your son become a machine, Eli? The human race is on track to become cyborgs within fifty years. Certainly, within your son's lifetime, if not your own. The human race needs to know this does not need to be their

Petra Nicoll

destiny. Every individual has free will, and every individual must execute it now."

"This is too much to process right now…I need to think about all this."

"Take your time. But not too much…" Michael nodded and stepped away, fading into the air like dust.

ELI TOOK ADVANTAGE of the solitude outdoors to hold a meditation session after the visit with Michael. His brain was highly active with programmed fear, confusion, and overwhelm. *I need to slow things down*, he thought.

Sitting up against the tree, with his legs crossed and his hands resting on his knees, he took several deep breaths before closing his eyes and sinking into the earth. He used a fourteen-breath technique called Tetrahedron Merkabah, which Angelina had taught him. The method allowed him to access his higher self, which he knew he needed at that moment.

At the end of the session, he felt in his heart that he needed to share all that he had learned from Michael—not just that day, but throughout the years of their relationship. But there were two people in particular whose opinions he still sought before he made a final decision. One of them stood before him, just as he opened his eyes.

"Dad," Eli smiled. "I was just thinking about you."

"Hello, Son. Yes, I thought you could use me now."

"So, you know all about what I now know?"

"Yes, of course. I knew much of this while I was still alive, you know."

"I didn't know…why didn't you ever say anything?"

"You would have thought I was crazy."

Eli laughed. "Yeah, you're probably right."

"I also knew you would carry the responsibility of exposing this truth to the world. My role was simply to raise you to the best of my ability so that when you reached adulthood you would have the strength to be who you were born to be."

"That's no simple task, Dad."

Robert chuckled. "Perhaps not simple, then. But the most rewarding thing I've ever done."

"So, you think I should reveal all of what's going on?"

"Absolutely. As you know in your heart."

"But what about Gabriel, Dad? Your grandson? Don't you fear for his life?"

"Of course, I want him to be safe. To be happy and healthy and to thrive. The same as I desire for all children. But if for some reason his life were to be cut short, it would not be in vain. Therefore, I encourage you not to fear what may happen to yourself or him, but to put one hundred percent conviction and faith in doing what you know needs to be done. If you believe in the power of what is right and good to prevail, then it will."

"Thanks, Dad. There is one more person I need to talk to about all of this first, though."

"May I suggest that there are two people? And they're both inside that house."

"You're right. I'll go tell them now. One of them won't be all that surprised…the other might call *me* crazy."

"If your mother is the latter, I assure you—she already knows."

"What? Mom knows about all of this?!"

"Maybe not all, but most. My Son, do you think your parents were just a couple of farmers?" Robert laughed.

"I'm beginning to question everything I've ever known."

"Good. As you should. By sharing what you know, you will lead a massive awakening that will cause everyone on your planet to question the same."

"Geez, I'm not sure I'm ready for that…"

"That is where you are wrong. You are ready, Son. Those who are ready to believe your truth will ascend to a higher plane of consciousness needed to survive. Those who are not ready will become—as Michael called them— 'cogs in the machine.'"

"Alright, Dad. Thanks for your help. I'm going to tell the ladies in the house now."

"Any time, Son. I love you."

"I love you too, Dad."

OF COURSE, ROBERT was right. Carol merely nodded along knowingly to everything Eli disclosed.

"So, what do you think, Mom? Should I reveal all of this?"

"Yes, of course, Eli. It is your responsibility. It is who your father and I raised you to be."

"And what do you think, Angelina? This affects you deeply, too. And of course, our son."

"Eli, you know the only right answer is the one that's in your heart. We may make some enemies, but although they could take our bodies, they could never take our souls. We will go on living, again and again—as individuals with free will."

Elizabeth had sat quietly throughout the whole conversation, with a look of complete shock on her face.

"Mom?" Angelina rested her hand upon her mother's. "Are you okay?"

"I…I think so. I mean, I am, it's just…" Elizabeth's eyes

darted around the room.

"What is it?"

"I…I used to have dreams about this. What Eli just described. Nightmares, really. While I was at the ashram. I thought it was just stress. After I moved here to the farm, the dreams stopped."

Angelina recalled some of her own nightmares, which were eerily similar to some of the scenarios Eli brought up, as well. "I used to have them, too, Mom. But they stopped when my subconscious started to realize I can choose an alternate reality than the one I witnessed in my dreams. I think the same thing happened to you."

"That makes sense. When I left your father and the ashram, I consciously chose a new reality for myself. That must have carried over into my subconscious."

"Now, we must collectively choose a new reality—all of the human race," Eli interjected. "We must do everything we can to spread this truth."

When Eli's publicist called the next day to confirm his interview with *Rolling Stone* magazine, he knew what he had to do.

"What are you going to tell them, Eli?" Angelina asked when he hung up the phone.

"Everything. I'm going to tell them everything."

CHAPTER THIRTEEN

<hr>

EVOLUTION

E li held the interview with *Rolling Stone* in the bedroom he grew up in. Never in a million years could he have imagined the experiences he'd have in his adult life, nor the words that would come out of his mouth in this interview. Michelle, the reporter was aghast as well; at times she was so silent Eli wasn't even sure she was still listening.

She probably thinks I'm a crazy person, he admitted to himself. It didn't matter to him, though; he knew he had a responsibility to be open and truthful. Aristotle was called crazy for saying the Earth was round, he reminded himself.

He started at the beginning with the story of how he first met Michael and held nothing back. He talked about Gemini and how various other secret societies promised your material wealth back in your next life, should you sign a sacred contract with them. "You understand reincarnation as a fact, right?" Eli had asked Michelle. "Um, yes, please continue," she replied. She did not want to interrupt Eli's flow with questions of her own. He talked about having visited Gemini's headquarters in L.A. and being shown to a room where he could see all of his past lives in one short film.

"In my most recent lifetime, I died with the promise that I would acquire $40 billion in my next life. I am nearly there—thanks to my career and various investments I've made, most importantly in cryptocurrencies. The traditional banking system is completely rigged, by the way. It's designed to keep all but the most elite leaders in society dependent on debt." Eli continued on to explain how cryptocurrencies work and how they would replace the dollar.

From there, he shared that he'd busted a sex trafficking ring in Thailand, and how many members of these secret societies—including many famous people and politicians—are involved in these rings. "I have a bounty on my head already, and it's only going to get more dangerous for me after this article comes out," Eli shared. "People have tried to kill me before—well, not really a 'person,' per se, but artificial intelligence—what I call a 'cyborg.' But I have to put the future of the human race and the planet before my own current incarnation."

"Tell me more about this…artificial intelligence? This… cyborg?" Michelle finally allowed herself to interject.

"Absolutely. Many humans have become cyborgs, actually. The entire human race is at risk of becoming cyborgs in the near future if we don't stop it. This article you're writing plays a role in that."

"How so?"

"Human behavior comes from perception, which comes from information received. The media, and especially popular culture, plays a very important role in informing—and manipulating—people's minds. If enough people are manipulated, humanity becomes enslaved in a reality that isn't real. Take, for instance, technology. Humans have become addicted to it, right? Can you imagine living without your smartphone? Your laptop? We have all become so attached to these devices that we carry them with us at all times.

"We have gone from these 'holdables' to 'wearables'—your Bluetooth and Google Glasses and Apple Watches—now to *injectables*. Thousands of people are getting micro-chipped—especially in Sweden and across Europe—with the sales pitch that when we permanently connect our bodies to artificial intelligence, we become superhuman. A tiny microchip placed under our skin allows us to conduct financial transactions, travel, and open locks on doors. But where doors can be opened, they can also be locked, right?

"At this point, we're connected to a global technological grid that can be centrally controlled by an elite few. We are therefore no longer human—we're cyborgs. We have no free will anymore. If the injector is under the control of the government, the government is then able to wipe out a whole class of people based on their beliefs or opposition to their agenda. A 'kill' mechanism can—and is already—part of this implantable. I know, because there is a cyborg pro-grammed to kill me."

"So…how do we evade all of this?"

"First, let me say that currently, powerful people in our government are seeking enlightened souls to 'steal.' There is a testing base at Area 51 in Nevada that is being used to ex-tract souls from humans and clone them, creating control-lable artificial intelligence cyborgs. So, the threat extends beyond manipulating humans through mind control and convincing them to consent to being microchipped, to ac-tual kidnapping—you are familiar with the extent of hu-man trafficking taking place in our world today, yes?"

"More or less, I know it's a problem…"

"It's a massive problem. There are an estimated 40 million slaves in the world today. About 10 million of these are children. Elite forces prey upon the most vulnerable. So, in answer to your question, we evade these problems by first waking up to the truth of their existence. We are beyond a point where we can cast off these issues as anomalies—they do not happen 'somewhere on the other side of the world' from us, they are happening right before our eyes. No doubt, people that you interact with every day are part of the problem. Music industry executives and performers are just as involved as film stars and banking executives and politicians."

"I don't know about that…"

"Believe it, Michelle. It's a hard truth, but the truth nonetheless."

"And by the way, while we're talking about music…music is one of the best ways to counteract these problems. Do you know why?"

"Why?"

"Because music, played in the right frequency, has an immense ability to heal. Have you ever been to one of my concerts?"

"To be honest, no I have not."

"Please, be my personal guest at my next gig. I'll connect you with my manager. You will witness for yourself how my music—especially when played live—can actually heal your body's cells. This is critically important now, with the expansion of 5G networks which, by the way, cause cancer and many other physical, mental, and even spiritual ailments.

"In regard to the latter, do you realize, Michelle, that

the earth is going through a profound transitional period?"

"Mmm…"

"Stay with me here. We are at the end of a twenty-five- or twenty-six-thousand-year cycle and are moving into a new age called the 'Age of Aquarius.' Surely, you're familiar with this concept from the popular song by that title. This is not a new concept, but people are waking up to it at a profound new pace—this era is one in which humanity is moving into a higher level of consciousness. Many sacred texts refer to this period, where people start to remember what they once knew. It is an exciting time to be on the planet if we make wise choices."

"Such as…?"

"Such as waking up to what's going on around us! If we truly pay attention, rather than distract ourselves with entertainment and technology and whatnot, we will see that full disclosure is underway. The old paradigm is crumbling and revealing the truth of our connection to the cosmos. Ours is not the only planet with intelligent life, but this fact has been conveniently kept from the masses in order to maintain a false reality that does not encourage personal growth, spirituality, and higher dimensional wisdom. To counteract that false reality, we must remember our own free will. We are not slaves to this machine, and we must refuse to let ourselves fall prey. We must also know that we can ask for help—the Galactic Federation is one Star Nation, in particular, that is here to help us awaken." Eli paused and registered silence.

"Michelle? Are you still with me?"

"I…uhhh…yes. I'm just…not sure we can publish all of this."

"May I suggest that—if you want the human race to

continue to exist—you must."

Everything happened at breakneck speed after that interview. Ron accompanied Eli, Angelina, and Gabriel back home to L.A. via plane the following day. Angelina had called Sara in advance and asked her to set up crystals throughout their home—for her own safety, as well as everyone else's.

The article in the *Rolling Stone* came out only two weeks later; it was not only the cover story but the longest feature in the magazine's history. Michelle shared with Eli that, although the publication was opening itself up to ridicule and even danger by sharing the full interview, the editorial team came to the conclusion that—with Eli being the level of rock star that he was—it was their responsibility to publish an authentic transcript of his words and his warnings. If it turned out to be false, the publicity the article would no doubt spark would sell millions of copies. If it turned out to be true...they may have just served as a catalyst for helping to save the human race.

"We're in all the way, either way," Michelle told him.

"Thank you. You won't regret it," Eli promised.

The immediate repercussions of the story were many—some of which Eli hadn't even given thought to. For one, the value of the dollar steadily began to deflate as millions of people diverted their money into cryptocurrencies. What this meant for early adopters such as Eli was that his wealth shot through the roof. Within three weeks, his net worth surpassed $45 billion. His initial shock at that number caused him to forget the significance of that milestone until Angelina reminded him over dinner at home one night after he shared the news from his estate manager.

"Love, $45 billion! Didn't you say your contract with Gemini was for $40 billion?"

"Ohmigod. I don't know how I could have forgotten… yes, it was. I guess I kind of expected lights to flash and some opening to a portal to appear before me when that happened," Eli laughed. "I mean, technically, that means I can die at any time now…I'm not protected by their personal investment in me."

"Don't look at it that way, that line of thinking will drive you crazy. What it really means is that you're not subject to their whims anymore. You're independent from them. You have your own free will. That's a good thing."

"Good point. But hey—that reminds me. I haven't had any encounter with that cyborg. I wonder if it's still programmed to kill me?"

"That's a good question for Michael…"

"True."

"What are you going to do with all that money, Eli?"

"That's another good question…not for Michael, but for my crypto buddies. We've been talking about supporting various fringe political candidates—and not just people running for president, but for elected positions across the House and Senate and local governments. We have to replace insider politicians currently in office, who have done nothing to stop and everything to perpetuate inequality in not only this country but around the world.

"That would be great. Imagine what all of your pooled wealth could accomplish…"

"We intend to force the abolishment of corporate donations in political campaigns, for one. And no more subsidies for the fossil fuel industry and pharmaceutical companies… we must establish a green economy. We have to ban 5G. We have to end human trafficking…"

"Seems like a tall order, but I have faith in you," Angelina came up behind Eli and wrapped her arms around his waist. Eli turned his head and kissed her cheek.

"You have always been my biggest supporter."

"You have always been mine. I have news to share, too," Angelina's voice rose with excitement as she came around to face Eli.

"You do? Tell me!"

"I heard from my agent today."

"And…?" Eli smiled in anticipation of what he felt she was going to share.

"Miracle Pictures is buying my screenplay. They want to make it a feature film!"

"*I knew it!* That's my woman! Now, will you let me read the damn thing?" Eli teased. Angelina had told him she didn't want to jinx it by sharing her script before it was pitched to her team.

"Yes, now you can read it."

Eli planted a big kiss on Angelina's mouth. "I'm so proud of you! Imagine how much exposure human trafficking is going to get after this film comes out. It's going to contribute to more people waking up to the truth."

"That's the intention. It's a timely topic—did you see the headlines in the paper today?"

"No, you know I don't read the paper much."

"This issue will interest you…" Angelina stood and retrieved the daily paper from the kitchen counter and brought it over to Eli.

"Leader of sex trafficking ring arrested, detained," Eli read the headline aloud. "Holy shit!" He continued reading the entire article, his mouth dropping further and further to the floor. "An undercover journalist exposed the highest tier of a sex trafficking ring based in Los Angeles last Friday. The ring has ties to several government officials and celebrities, whose names will be revealed as details of the case are released to the public. The bust was the result of the journalist's covert participation in a recruitment event for a secret society by the name of Gemini…" Eli paused from reading. "Ohmigod! Gemini is being implicated!"

"Incredible, isn't it? Just when your contract was concluded, too," Angelina acknowledged.

"Thankfully, I didn't sign another one under my name. The name Derek Stryker will mean nothing to officials."

"It will be very interesting to see whose names do come up."

"I agree. This could lead to a whole new organization of government leaders…many of them will be arrested, if they haven't been already. This is huge…I think I need to talk to Michael about this."

Angelina could feel the urgency in his voice. "Go for it. I'll be upstairs putting Gabriel to sleep."

"Thanks, Ang. I'll be downstairs in my studio." Eli kissed the top of Angelina's head and ran downstairs, quietly closing the glass door behind him. He didn't need privacy to call on Michael, but he was able to center himself better when he was alone.

Sinking into his favorite chair, he took a deep breath and opened his mouth to speak, "Mic—"

"Yes?" Michael appeared on the couch before Eli even finished saying his name.

"Oh, hey. I should have known you'd be ready for me."

"I anticipated you might have some questions. A lot has transpired as of late, has it not?"

"That's an understatement."

"And, there's more to it than is in the news."

"That's what I figured. Clue me in, Michael. What all is going on with the arrest of this ring leader? And what does this mean for Gemini?"

"Well, what hasn't made the news yet is that the leader of this ring, in an attempt to destroy all evidence of his involvement, set fire to his office immediately before his arrest. This wasn't a standard 'office,' however—it was a programming center for AI. Including...can you guess?

"No, tell me."

"The cyborg that was programmed to kill you. Convenient news, is it not? You're off the hook, kid."

"Wait, so that creepy guy isn't after me anymore?"

"Nope. The control panel has been destroyed. I am guessing the media is going to take some time before revealing that information—the general public is still adapting to the idea that this type of AI exists. But that's not all, Eli. It gets even better..."

"Tell me!"

"That *Rolling Stone* article set all this in motion...when it became clear that Gemini was going to be investigated, many of its members stormed the building and destroyed their contracts to obliterate record of their own involvement. Do you understand what this means?"

"Well...if that was the only record of their contracts... does that make them obsolete?"

"Indeed."

"So, that means they are not guaranteed wealth in their next life?"

"Correct. And because of that, can you guess what they will most likely decide to do?"

"Whoa…not reincarnate?"

"Exactly. They don't want to start back over as poor people in their next life. They would have an awful lot of bad karma to tend to."

"My god…this is massive."

"I thought you'd see so. This is an incredible opportunity for humanity to evolve. And, Eli? Do you recognize the role you have played in all of this?"

"Umm, well I guess."

"Your response tells me that you do not. You can pat yourself on the back for a job extremely well done. What you shared with *Rolling Stone* would not have been taken seriously—by the magazine, nor by the public—had you not worked so hard to build a reputable career and following. Your music would not have healed the bodies and souls of billions of people that have attended your concerts and listened to your songs. You have contributed to the evolution of this planet and its people on an epic scale. And, Eli, you have already created one child who will carry on the work you have started long after your current life has ended. You have yet to witness the depth of what he will be capable of as he grows older. I assure you, it's a beautiful thing. He will make you very proud, just as you have made your parents proud. And me, too, Eli."

"Aww, stop. You're going to make me cry."

"Don't let my presence stop you."

"Honestly, Michael, I couldn't have done any of this without you. I was just a naïve, lost kid when you took me under your wing. Or, should I say, when you scared the shit out of me by warping out of a mirror?"

Michael laughed. "I had to catch your attention somehow."

"All kidding aside, you've been extremely patient with me. You've taught me so much…"

"When the student is ready, the teacher appears, isn't that what they say? Your parents did a great job preparing you for me. And someone else, too."

"Angelina."

Michael smiled. "Yes, Angelina."

"I owe her so much…"

"I don't want to speak for her, but I don't think she would see it that way. I believe she was looking for you, too."

"Yes, maybe you're right," Eli smiled. He suddenly had the urge to run upstairs and wrap her in his arms.

"Go on," Michael read his mind. "You are through with me here."

"I hope you don't mean forever, Michael?"

"That is up to you. I believe you hold the power within yourself to find the answers you need from here on out. But of course, I am always here if you need me."

"Thank you. For everything."

"My pleasure," Michael grinned and brought his hand to his head in a salute before evaporating into the air.

Eli took a few deep breaths to integrate everything that he had just learned and reflected on the history he had shared with Michael. *I'm going to miss that old guy,* he thought. He wiped away a tear brimming his eye. *I know he will still be around, but something tells me our relationship will never quite be the same.* Eli said a prayer of gratitude, then made his way up the two flights of stairs to the nursery.

There, he found Angelina standing over Gabriel's crib.

"Shhh." Angelina smiled as she held a finger to her mouth and whispered, "I just got him to sleep."

Eli wrapped his arms around her waist and rested his chin on her shoulder. Together, they stood over their child, a growing boy now of eighteen months.

"He's beautiful. Like his mother," Eli brushed Angelina's thick, dark hair aside and kissed her neck. Angelina placed her hand on top of his.

"Like his father," she kissed his cheek.

At that moment, Eli had an idea. "Hey, Ang?" he said excitedly.

"Yes?" Angelina kept her voice low.

"I know we've talked about marriage and a wedding not being important to us, but what do you think about having a spiritual ceremony? A sort of public declaration of our love and our union? I feel like we should honor how far we've come together, and how much we mean to each other. You mean so much to me, Ang. I do hope you know that."

"Aww, of course, I do." Angelina kissed him again. "If that is something you'd like to do, I support that. Our mothers would be beyond happy," she laughed.

"How about holding it on the island in the Caribbean? The one where I had my spiritual awakening...you know, after we broke up because I was too young and stupid for a woman of your caliber?" He winked.

Angelina laughed. "Well, I wouldn't say 'stupid.' But you did have some growing up to do."

"Something is growing on me now," Eli smiled devilishly and pressed his body up against hers.

"Oh, please," Angelina laughed. "Aren't we beyond corny sex lines by now? If you want to make love to me, just bring me to the bedroom."

"I don't think I can make it there," Eli smiled. "How about the hallway?"

"Deal," Angelina had barely said the word before Eli swooped her off her feet and carried her to the hall, quietly closing the nursery door behind them. Their hearts both began to race as Eli rested Angelina's backside on the railing. He reached his hand under her silk nightgown, softly caressing the folds of her labia with his forefinger.

"I love it when you're not wearing any panties," he whispered with a heavy breath. "You're so warm…" Angelina responded by inserting her tongue deeper inside Eli's mouth, then working her way around his lips.

"Your lips are so soft…" she replied.

"So are yours," Eli continued to run his finger along the inside of her sacred opening, feeling the dampness and heat inside of her. He could feel the throbbing of his own sexual member as it fought to break free from his jeans. Angelina reached down and undid the top button of his pants with her hands and used her feet to bring them to the floor.

"Mmm…perfect height. Why haven't we used the railing before?" Eli grinned. He brought himself closer in and needed no assistance as he entered the woman he loved with ease.

"I love you," he whispered in her ear.

"I love you too, Eli," Angelina's chin lifted higher as she threw her head back against the wall. Sweat formed on her brow and began to run down toward her chest. Eli leaned forward and licked the salty stream of moisture that was now flowing between her breasts.

Angelina placed her hands on his head, holding tightly onto his thick blonde hair. "Harder," she moaned.

"As you wish," Eli smiled, panting heavily as he moved deeper and deeper inside of her. He fought to keep himself from coming, wanting her to experience the height of her pleasure first. He gently stroked her clitoris with each penetration while stimulating her nipples with his tongue, knowing exactly what she loved.

"*Ohhh...*" Angelina's moan affirmed his success.

"*Shhh,* you'll wake the baby," Eli teased. He shouldn't have been so brazen; moments later, a guttural moan escaped his own mouth, the likes of which he'd never heard come out of himself before.

Angelina giggled, high on endorphins. "Good job, love."

Eli collapsed against her on the wall, too exhausted to respond. Angelina slid down from the railing and embraced him.

"You deserve to be tired," she reached up and held his face in her hands, looking into his eyes. "After all, you *did* just awaken all of humanity."

Eli released a deep sigh. "Somebody had to do it," he grinned. "Why not a rock star?"

www.ingramcontent.com/pod-product-compliance
Lightning Source LLC
Chambersburg PA
CBHW031202260626
47169CB00004B/1212